Nightmare Stories

Matthew Dewar

This is a work of fiction. All of the characters, organisations, and events portrayed in this book are either products of the author's imagination or used fictitiously.

No part of this book may be used or reproduced in any manner whatsoever without written permission, except in the case of brief quotations embodied in critical articles or reviews.

For information, contact:

https://matthewdewarauthor.wordpress.com

ISBN: 978-0-648-07990-3

To my brother, Harrison
Reading isn't the nightmare you make it out to be

TABLE OF CONTENTS

Neighbours from Hell

Travis doodled on his notepad while his teacher droned on about calculating the area of a triangle. *Half base times height. How hard is it for people to understand?* He allowed his mind to wander, jumping in his chair when the bell went off. As people raced out of the classroom, one student hovered in front of Travis' desk.

"You shouldn't be drawing stuff like that." Nick lifted his backpack higher on his shoulder and walked out the classroom.

Travis glanced down at his drawing. He couldn't even remember what he had been doodling. It was only an upside-down star that he had circled. Nothing rude or bad. *What was Nick's problem?*

Nick was a weird kid and hadn't made an effort to make any friends since he moved here last year. Anyone who did try and be nice to him was shot down with a snide remark or his trademark creepy stare. Travis shrugged off the weird encounter and waved goodbye to Mr Brinkley on the way out of the classroom.

It was Friday afternoon. Laughter and excitement bounced around the usually sombre halls. Nick fell into step with Travis as he walked down the corridor among the throngs of happy kids heading home for the weekend. Travis shot Nick a sidelong glance. "Um, hey?"

"I saw what you drew in class."

"And?" Travis said. "It was just a star. I was bored."

Nick studied Travis long and hard. "Just a star. Really?"

"Yeah, just a star."

Nick's black hair fell in front of his eyes and he brushed it behind his ear. His fingernails were painted midnight black and were chipped around the edges.

A flash of silver caught Travis' attention. A chain hung around Nick's neck with an upside down five pointed star circled by a snake. The points of the star had little glittering stones embedded in the metal; a small pinprick of red, blue, yellow, purple and green.

"Hey, your necklace. It's just like the star I drew." Travis pointed at it.

Nick shook his head and lowered his voice. "Not a star, a pentagram."

They stepped outside into the cold winter chill of June and Travis pulled the hood of his jumper up over his head and zipped it up to his neck. He really hoped Nick would leave him alone. The guy was making him uncomfortable with his staring and air of self-importance.

Travis sighed as Nick continued to walk with him. "Don't you have somewhere to go?"

"Yeah." He shrugged and continued walking.

Travis stopped in his tracks and turned to face Nick. "Are you following me?"

Nick scoffed. "Please. I've got better things to do with my life than follow you. I'm walking home. Is that okay with you or would you rather I go the long way?"

Travis' cheeks warmed with embarrassment. He mumbled an apology and continued walking.

Nick followed Travis in silence as they left school and traipsed along the pathway that led through a park and over to the side of town where Travis lived.

Eventually, Nick spoke. "So, got any plans for tonight?"

Travis couldn't believe his ears. The kid who hardly said boo to anyone was engaging him in small talk. "Um, I'm just going to go home and play some Playstation." He hoped Nick wouldn't ask for an invite. "What about you?"

A smile played at the edges of Nick's mouth. "Dad's been working away for the last twelve months and he's finally coming home, so we're having a party."

"Is he in the army or something?" Travis asked.

"Something like that." Nick fingered the star shaped pendant on his necklace. "So what are you doing later tonight, it *is* the winter solstice after all."

"That's the shortest day of the year, right?" Travis scratched the back of his head. "I don't see how my life will be any different because of it."

Nick appeared disappointed. "So, you really were just doodling in class today, weren't you? That pentagram doesn't mean anything to you?"

Travis shook his head.

"And you don't think there's anything special about the winter solstice?"

"Nope."

"Okay." Nick fell into silence, the only sound coming from the leaves crunching under their shoes. After a while, he removed the chain from around his neck and held it out for Travis. "Here, I want you to have this."

"No. I don't want it." Travis couldn't work out what this kid's deal was.

"Please, just take it. You can give it back to me later." Nick's eyes glistened.

"Fine. If it means that much to you." Travis shrugged and took the necklace.

Nick winked. "See you later!" He quickened his pace down the street.

Travis slowed down a bit to increase the distance between himself and Nick. He was such a strange kid. He turned the pendant over in his hands. *Why did Nick give this to me?* Not wanting to lose it, he put it around his neck.

Lost in thought, Travis continued walking home. He was shocked to find out that Nick was approaching a house on his street. How had he never noticed that before?

Nick walked up to the run-down house a few doors down from Travis' place. The grass was overgrown and an old blue ute was slowly rusting away in the driveway. The front security screen hung at an angle off one hinge and most of the windows were covered with tin foil. Travis had always assumed that the house was vacant as he never saw anyone come or go. But once every year, the house came alive with weird noises, and most of the neighbourhood claimed it was haunted.

Travis jogged up his own driveway, adjacent to their perfectly manicured lawns, and hurried inside. Their house was pristine, inside and out, and Travis wondered what the inside of Nick's house looked like if the outside was as run-down as it was.

All thoughts of Nick vanished as Travis eyed his new car racing game for his PlayStation. He had already unlocked a few of the base model cars, and with a bit more progress, he'd have access to faster cars and better maps.

He tipped a bag of popcorn into a bowl, poured himself a tall glass of chocolate milk and sat down in front of the TV.

Travis expertly controlled his Nissan Skyline GT-R through the city streets on the map. He avoided collisions, and almost lost control once, but he still won. Several races later, his dad's car rumbled into the driveway.

"Hello?" Travis' dad called from the front door. "Travis. Come help me with dinner."

Travis paused the game and ran to the front door, taking a plastic bag of food off his father's hands. Friday night Chinese had become a ritual for the two of them after deciding that neither of their cooking was safe to eat. For a while, Travis' mum had made a casserole or something before going to night shift at the hospital, but Travis's dad soon decided he'd rather have takeout, despite his growing waistline.

Travis flicked on the lights as he set the table and put the food in the middle for them to share. Fried rice, honey chicken, satay beef and a big bag of prawn crackers. All their favourites.

Travis had just piled his plate up when his dad entered the room, his tie loosened and top button undone.

"Hey, Dad, guess what?"

"What?" his dad said, dishing up a plate for himself.

"That house on the end of the street isn't vacant after all. One of the kids I go to school with lives there."

Travis' dad furrowed his eyebrows. "That can't be right. The bank bought it back from the owners several months ago and they have plans to demolish and rebuild it later this year."

Travis put his fork down. "But I saw one of the kids from school go inside."

"They might have just been exploring the house. I know the rumours about it being haunted. But it is dangerous. I'll speak to my manager tomorrow and suggest he put up a temporary fence or something to keep kids out." He scratched his chin. "I don't want you going there, okay?"

Travis shrugged. "I wasn't going to. The kid that went inside is a bit weird." Travis piled a prawn cracker high with fried rice and shoved the whole thing in his mouth, barely managing to stuff it all in there. He thought about Nick and wondered if he was just showing off. Why else would he have gone into that house?

Friday nights weren't just about the Chinese takeout. A movie marathon always followed dinner. Every Friday, Travis and his father would take turns picking a movie. They plopped down on the couch to watch his dad's choice: *Butch Cassidy and the Sundance Kid.*

As the end credits rolled, Travis made his way to the bathroom and brushed his teeth. When he changed into his pyjamas, he remembered the chain around his neck. He contemplated taking it off, but for some reason decided to leave it on. Snuggling up under the warm covers on his bed, he was asleep in an instant. Dreams of him and his father robbing a train and riding off on horses into the sunset, laughing and filthy rich, filled his head.

Travis woke later that night to rain pattering down on their roof, which was strange because he vaguely remembered the weather forecaster saying they were in for a dry, but cold, couple of days. Over the rain, an odd chanting noise could be heard from outside. Nick's pendant was warm against Travis' skin. He tiptoed through the house, past his snoring father, and peered out between the curtains of the front window.

A thick plume of smoke rose up out of the chimney of the supposedly vacant house and joined the swirling dark clouds above. Lights danced in between the strips of tin foil that covered the windows. The chanting sound was definitely coming from there, but also seemed to bounce about inside Travis' skull. The words were indecipherable: definitely not

English. Nick and his family were obviously throwing his dad a really weird welcome home party.

Lightning forked the sky and struck the TV aerial on Nick's roof, sending sparks flying. A loud crack of thunder boomed through the night. In the other room, Travis' father snorted, before resuming his steady snoring rhythm.

The rain slowed to a light drizzle and despite his father's warning, Travis' curiosity got the better of him.

He threw on a waterproof jacket and a pair of shoes before grabbing his key from the rack by the door. He placed it safely in his pocket then left the warm house, stepping outside into the chill.

Wind whipped through his hair and he pulled the jacket around himself tighter before shoving his hands in his pockets. He jogged to warm himself up a bit.

Peeking through the slits in the tin foil covered windows, Travis couldn't see much of what was going on inside. He went around to the front door and as he reached out to see if it was unlocked, the door opened.

"I knew you'd come." Nick beamed at Travis.

"What's going on?" Travis asked.

"Come inside, I'll show you."

Travis remembered his father's warning. He was just about to walk away when the pendant around his neck started burning. It zapped him, and all thoughts about leaving vanished. Travis entered.

Standing on the front landing, Travis was about to take his jacket off when he remembered he was only wearing his pyjamas underneath. Nick stood beside him wearing a long black robe with a hood that cast his face in shadows. He beckoned Travis deeper into the house and although the hairs on the back of his neck stood on edge, Travis followed.

When he walked through to the main living area, Travis' jaw dropped.

A large chalk star had been drawn on the wooden floorboards. There were others already in the room, each person standing on one point of the star, with the fifth point empty. They all wore the same dark robe as Nick and chanted in low voices. They could have been speaking gibberish, or a foreign language. Whatever it was, Travis was confused. Candles and incense burned all around. The air was thick with a pungent smell of something earthy and sweet. Solid lines of salt covered the windowsills and doorframes.

Travis opened his mouth but the pendant zapped him again. He forgot what he was about to say.

Nick took Travis' hand and led him into the middle of the room. Travis was about to resist when the pendant zapped him once more. Travis followed Nick like a puppy dog.

When Travis stood in the centre of the star, Nick took the pendant back from him.

As the pendant left his touch, Travis seemed to wake up. "Nick, what's going on?" He tried to step outside the middle of the chalk pentagram, but a shimmering wall of air solidified around the edges, trapping him inside.

Nick smiled sadly at Travis and left him standing there, taking his place at the unoccupied point of the star and joined the chanting with the others.

Travis tested the glimmering barrier once more, but it was as solid as a brick wall, sending a shiver of electricity through him.

The five cloaked people, including Nick, mouthed the words of their chant and swayed their bodies to and fro. Their lips moved faster and faster. Candles flickered and their robes fluttered about their ankles.

Travis' heart pounded in his chest and his eyes watered. "Nick! Stop!"

The ground beneath his feet shuddered, and cracks appeared on the surface of the floorboards. Two boards fractured and split open at the joint and Travis jumped aside to avoid the wood piercing his feet. The candles around the room flared brilliantly, flames licking upwards towards the ceiling.

The floorboards turned to ash, before the charred flakes dissolved into the air. Travis lost his breath as he looked down at his feet to see he was standing on top of nothing. His stomach back-flipped. A deep, dark crevice had opened up and plunged down into the depths of the earth as far as his eye could see.

A pair of glowing red embers crept towards him out of the darkness.

Travis screamed over the pounding of his heart.

Not embers. Eyes!

Eyes that were sunken in a ram's skull with huge curled horns. The monster's body belonged to a man with a chiselled muscular torso and thick, splintered black fingernails.

Travis yelled at the people in the room who had now fallen silent. "Help me!" He pounded on the walls of his prison. What was Nick doing to him?

The ram-headed man clawed his way out of the pit, rising to tower over Travis in the confined space. "Hi, I'm Darryl," he said in a cheerful voice.

Travis' vision went blurry for a moment. His hands shook violently at his sides. "T, T, Travis," he stammered.

"Nice to meet you, T, T, Travis," he said. His long fingernails scratched at the skin around his neck. "Don't worry, the summoning is almost over."

"Summoning?" Travis asked.

"They did a good job with the pentagram," Darryl observed, studying the chalk drawing around their feet.

Travis couldn't wrap his mind around what was going on. Was this some kind of devil worshipping, demon summoning ritual? Why was he involved?

The floorboards returned underneath his feet and the solid walls of air dispersed as one of the hooded figures struck a gong.

Travis' nose tickled then he sneezed from the strong smell of cinnamon and sandalwood in the air.

Nick rushed towards the ram-headed man and embraced him in a hug. "Dad! It's so good to see you."

Travis looked between Nick and the ram-headed man like he was at a tennis tournament. "Dad?"

Nick nodded his head proudly and the other four people removed their hoods. "This is my family," Nick said. He pointed to each in turn. An older woman with black hair pulled up into a bun was his mum. Two identical looking older teenagers were his twin brothers and the smallest of the lot was his younger sister. "And, of course, this is my dad."

"Of course he's your dad." Travis smiled awkwardly. "Of course this is all real."

Nick's dad removed the ram's skull from his shoulders and placed it on the dirty kitchen counter. "Ah, after twelve months, it feels good to take that cursed thing off." He looked over at Travis. "And I think it'll be a good fit." He patted Nick on the shoulder. "Good job, son."

"Good fit? Sorry, what?" Travis took a few back steps before he bumped into the twins.

Nick nodded. "Dad's year is up. We had to find someone to replace him."

"Replace him? What do you mean?" Travis wiped his sweaty hands on his pyjama bottoms, his shallow breaths were raspy.

Darryl sighed. "Didn't you tell him anything?"

Nick shook his head. "I didn't have time. Sorry, Dad."

Darryl ruffled his son's hair. "That's alright." He waved Travis over. "Come here."

Travis' feet were quite happy where they were, but the twins pushed him closer. They held his shoulders still while Darryl placed the ram's skull on Travis' shoulders. Darryl stepped back to admire Travis' new look. "See, what did I tell you? Perfect fit."

Travis lost his peripheral vision the moment the skull covered his face. His world was reduced to the two small eye holes. Travis tried to pull the ram's head off, but it wouldn't budge. His neck itched where the ram's head should have ended, but there was no seam. It had melded with his own skin somehow.

Darryl flourished his hands in front of Travis. "Behold: Travis. Hell's newest customer service manager."

Nick's family applauded, big grins plastered on their faces.

Darryl leant in close to Travis. "I'm sorry, kiddo. It's a tough job. People always have something to complain about down there." He put on a high-pitched mocking voice. "It's too hot. My chains are too tight. My torture is too painful." His voice returned to his normal gruff tone. "Ugh. I'm sick of it. I'm glad my shift is finally over and Nick's found someone to replace me."

"Replace you? For how long?"

"Not long." Darryl shrugged. "It's a twelve-month contract. This house is a gateway to the Underworld. At the next winter solstice, a family or friend of yours can come, perform the summoning and get someone to replace you."

Travis let out a pitiful moan. "But my dad doesn't know where I am."

"Don't worry." Nick clapped him on the back. "I'll be here waiting for you with someone else to take your place. It's not like this house is going anywhere."

The pentagram in the centre of the room burst into flames and the floorboards charred away to nothing.

"No!" Travis screamed. "The bank! They're going to demolish the house."

Darryl flinched. "That sucks kid. I'm really sorry."

"But, but, but," Travis stammered.

A bullwhip cracked the air and latched onto the horn on the side of Travis' head. A bone-trembling roar rose out from the ground.

"Looks like your boss is ready for you to start work. He acts tough but he's a real softie. Good luck!" Darryl waved as Travis was pulled down into the depths of the underworld by his new horn.

On Crystal Clear Waters

Sunlight reflected off the ocean as Jack and his dad zipped across the water. The small boat's engine let out a high-pitched whine as they bounced from wave to wave, causing cold sea spray to splash Jack's face.

Patches of light turquoise water blended into the murky dark areas beyond them. The sea swelled underneath in a rhythmical seesaw motion. Off in the distance, waves crashed against a reef, spewing white foam and bubbles on the surface.

Jack's dad slowed the boat and leaned over to check the GPS and ultrasonic fish scanner. He killed the engine and they drifted according to the wont of the ocean. Turning to Jack, he grinned. "This place looks like a good spot. Here, give me a hand with the anchor."

There was no noise, save for the gentle slap of water against the hull and the occasional squawk from a lone seagull. Jack hated the noisy mechanical shriek the engine made, but now it had stopped, he drank in the peace of being on the water.

"Take in a big whiff of that clean air and ocean smell." Jack's dad inhaled deeply through his nose.

Jack was just about to when—

Brrrrp.

Jack's dad cracked up.

Gagging, Jack pinched his nose shut. "That's gross!" There was something about the smell of farts that made Jack want to throw up. Fortunately, the wind quickly cleared the stinky smell.

The boat pitched to the side as Jack stood to help his dad lift the anchor and throw it overboard. The chain rattled against the metal railing then disappeared, trailing a long line of rope that was tied to the bow.

Jack's dad opened one of the buckets and pulled out a packet of bait. He tore it open and the strong, pungent smell assaulted Jack's nostrils. Within a few seconds though, his nose adjusted and he relaxed.

His dad hooked a hunk of squid on the end of a line and handed it to Jack. "Remember what I told you about casting?"

"Yep." Jack nodded. He lifted the bail arm and took the rod behind him, then flicked it forward and watched the baited end of the line fly out about twenty metres in front of him.

"Not bad," his dad remarked.

Jack waited for the reel to stop letting line out and flipped the bail arm back down again. The sinker had hit the bottom of the ocean, and he had to wait for the first bite. He pressed his finger lightly against the thin line, feeling for any vibrations that would mean fish were interested in his bait.

"Any bites?" his dad asked.

Jack shook his head. "Nah, not yet."

Jack watched in amazement as his father cast his line out twice as far as he had managed, before leaning back against the hull of the boat and putting his feet up.

They sat for several minutes without any bites, and the initial excitement started to wear Jack's patience thin. The sun beat down on him hard, cooking his skin. He wondered how much longer he could last before he needed to slop on more sunscreen.

Finally, Jack felt a tug on his line; a small bite at first, then a rapid triple nibble. On the fifth bite, he yanked his rod upwards and hooked the fish. The muscles in his left forearm burned as he gripped the rod tightly, his right hand working the reel handle as fast as he could.

"You're doing well! Keep it up!" his dad cheered.

The top of the rod was bent almost in half. Whatever fish he had caught was going to be huge!

"Let it out a bit. Tire it out." His dad hovered around Jack with twitching fingers. "Do you want me to take over?"

"Nup. I go this." Jack did as he was told. He reeled the fish in for several seconds, then allowed the fish some time to swim away, then repeated. "Why did I have to cast my line so far away?" Jack jokingly complained.

"Come on, you're nearly there." His dad drummed his fingers on the edge of the boat. "A few more minutes and we'll have dinner in our hands."

At that moment, his Dad's rod went berserk. The line was pulled mightily and his Dad cheered. "I've got one too!" He pulled his rod out of the holder and began reeling in his own catch.

Jack hoped his was better and bigger than his father's. His family wasn't overly competitive, but Jack had always strived to be the best.

A shadow down below grew closer, gaining in size, looking like a big hulk of a fish. Until the shadow no longer resembled a fish. It was a boot. Jack almost let out a sob. His arms burned, his back ached and he had failed miserably. Meanwhile, a giant fish thrashed about just under the surface as Jack's dad brought in his catch.

Jack's dad grimaced. "Hey, sorry bud. These things happen. Can you come here and help me with this one? I don't wanna lose him."

Frustrated, Jack grabbed the net his father nodded to and picked it up. He leaned over the side of the boat and scooped the net under the fish. Together, they pulled it in.

It was a giant silver beast, with black tiger stripes along its body, the top half of its scaly skin was coloured an almost metallic blue.

"A Spanish mackerel!" his dad cheered. "And a big one!" He placed the fish into the large esky full of sea water. "This is awesome!" He clapped his hands together.

He turned to his son, his smile fading as he patted Jack on the shoulder. "Hey, it's okay. We don't want to overfish these waters, anyway. We should only catch what we can reasonably consume. No more."

Jack smiled at that. He gave the boot a once over. "I thought catching boots while fishing was a joke. I didn't realise people actually caught them. What's a boot doing out here anyway?"

His dad shrugged. "A lot of rubbish ends up in the ocean, and all the world's oceans are connected. Currents drag items around the place all the time. Sometimes trash can damage reefs and kill wildlife. That's why you should never litter." He took a drink from a water bottle before offering it to Jack. "But you never know, that could even be from a shipwreck."

Jack took the bottle and downed several big mouthfuls. He turned the boot over in his hands and noticed a name scratched into the sole of the boot. *This be the property of Captain Gasspantz.*

Jack chuckled at the name and dropped the boot at his feet. He'd throw it away properly when they got back to shore.

"Hey, now we've caught enough fish for dinner, how about we go for a snorkel? It looks like there's a good reef down there. And you never know, we might find some sunken treasure!"

Jack peered down into the dark water. He hated going swimming in the ocean where he couldn't see the bottom. "Can we go back to the shallow waters? What if there's a shark down there?"

"The ocean's huge. The chances of us seeing a shark are slim to none. Did you know, you've got more of a chance of dying from a coconut falling on your head than you do of getting eaten by a shark?"

Jack gazed up at the sky. "Do you see any coconut trees around here? There could be sharks down there though." He pointed to the water.

"Fine. Stay in the boat then. I'm going snorkelling. Unless you want to get over your fear?" His dad's challenge hung in the air.

His dad had already beat him at fishing. Jack couldn't live with the shame of being too scared to swim as well, so he changed into his swimmers, put his flippers on, and then his snorkel and mask.

Sliding into the water, Jack blew out a huge lungful of air as the frigid water enveloped him. Goosebumps bristled all over his body and he rubbed his arms to try and warm up. He broke the surface and breathed through the snorkel. His dad splashed into the water next to him and together they swam around, Jack's eyes constantly darting around on the lookout for would-be predators.

The reef was an impressive structure of coral, seaweed and hundreds of little fish zipping around. The multicoloured fish poked their heads out between fronds of weeds, before shooting away whenever Jack or his father swam too close.

Jack's dad pointed out a stingray gliding along lazily, and later a bright orange starfish attached to a hunk of brown coral. Jack kept his fingers far away from a fluorescent yellow and green sea cucumber that was almost definitely poisonous.

A dark cave loomed ahead. Something resembling writhing black tentacles shifted within its inky depths and a giant red eye cracked open to peer at Jack. A cold shiver ran down his body and he almost swallowed a mouthful of water.

Blinking, Jack cleared his vision and looked again. Nothing there. Just some seaweed and oddly shaped rocks. He scolded himself for being such a scaredy cat.

Jack scanned the glistening sand along the bottom of the ocean for anything that could be associated with the boot: evidence of a shipwreck, golden coins, a diamond necklace, or maybe even a giant ruby.

Jack dove down to the bottom and ran his hands through sand that was made up of billions of crushed shells, kicking up a cloud of dust that temporarily obscured his vision.

His dad was behind him to the right somewhere. As Jack prepared to kick off from the bottom and get another lungful of air, a dark shadow passed in front of him. His blood pounded in his ears. Could it be a shark?

He raced to the surface. As his head poked out of the water, he caught his breath. He eyed the boat not too far away and powered through the water towards it.

He prayed it was a dolphin, or just his mind playing tricks on him again, but he couldn't be sure. He needed to get out of the water!

His father was over by the reef, looking deep into the cave. Jack wouldn't go near anything like that, even though he knew the giant octopus thing was just a trick of his imagination. He preferred the open water where any predators would be seen long before they tried to eat him.

Jack caught movement to his left. The shark! He froze in the water, fear gripping him in a bear-hug. But the tail was wrong; it was shaped more like a dolphin's. He spun around in circles, trying to get a look at what was swimming around him, just beyond his vision.

He stopped spinning and quickly turned the other way, catching sight of a girl.

No ... a mermaid!

Her beautiful golden hair floated around her head like a halo. Sunlight caught the individual scales of her powerful aquamarine tail. She smiled at him with plump red lips, her light green eyes twinkling with curiosity.

She giggled and wiggled her finger at Jack, beckoning him to swim closer.

Without realising what he was doing, Jack drifted towards the mermaid as she sang, his heart melting like butter, entranced by her beautiful melody.

He swam towards her and every time he got close enough to touch her, she'd swim further away before turning and calling him again. He desperately wanted to know where she was leading him. *Maybe to sunken treasure?*

Up ahead, the ocean floor plummeted so far down, even the light filtering through the water couldn't reach the bottom. Jack shivered as his mind conjured up images of what creatures could be lurking in the dark depths below. Whatever treasure was down there could stay down there.

The mermaid swam towards him, smiling sweetly with a flash of her pearly white teeth. A soft, delicate hand reached out for his, washing away his fears of what dangers might be hiding just out of sight. Jack knew in his heart that she wouldn't let anything bad happen to him.

He extended his hand for hers.

In a split second, everything about her changed. Soft skin turned hard and scaly. Her pearly whites turned to sharp yellow needles and her hands grew webbed and spiny with long claws at the end of each finger.

Jack almost inhaled a lungful of water. He was suffocating; he hadn't taken a breath of fresh air in a long time now. His ribs burned. He tried to swim away as fast as he could.

The mermaid was a much faster swimmer, and before Jack turned around, her hand latched around his ankle and dragged him down.

He kicked wildly but her webbed grip was too strong. She dragged him deeper into the colder and darker water, claws digging into his skin. Her sweet, soft song that had enticed him to swim after her had turned into a cackling, hacking, cough-like noise.

Jack's vision turned blurry. Spots danced at the edges of his vision. He almost thought he saw a huge wooden ship sail above him on the surface.

Something large splashed into the water, and raced directly for Jack.

A large hunk of an anchor careened past him and smacked the mermaid straight in the face. It dragged her down to the bottom of the sea bed.

But her hand still gripped Jack's ankle tightly and he was dragged down deeper with her. The pressure from the water pressed in all around him, making his ears scream in pain.

Jack kicked and squirmed. Black dots flashed before his eyes. Finally, he kicked himself free of her death-grip. His lungs were about to implode. It felt like an elephant was sitting on his chest. He swam to the surface, as fast as he could. His need for fresh air far outweighed the risk of getting the bends.

Jack broke the surface with seconds to spare before he blacked out. He spent several moments sucking in air and recovering, before he remembered what had happened and searched for the boat that had saved his life with its anchor.

He looked behind him and choked at the sight of a colossal wooden ship with a pirate flag flapping in the breeze. The words 'The Borborygmus' were painted in white on the lichen covered hull.

"Argh! There be the young lad that taken me boot!" A pirate with a black hat and a parrot on his shoulder pointed at Jack. His bushy red beard waved in the wind.

The crew stood beside him on the ship. They all sported beards and looked like they could use a shower. Some had patches over their eyes or golden hoops dangling from their ears. One had a peg over his nose.

Jack swam away from the ship as fast as he could. He spied their boat and raced towards it, hoping his dad was already on board and ready to go.

The pirate gasped. "He's headed fer his ship. Don't let him get away!"

Jack had closed half the gap between the pirate ship and his dad's dinghy when a cannonball whistled through the air and crashed into their family boat.

Jack stopped and treaded water, watching his father's pride and joy slowly sink to the bottom of the water. Now Jack prayed his dad wasn't already on the boat.

A pirate dove into the water and swam past Jack. He ducked under and resurfaced several seconds later with the boot extended above his head. "I've got yer boot, cap'n," he called.

The pirates on the ship all cheered.

"Good. 'N bring the boy," the captain called in his gruff tone.

A rope was tossed out from the ship and the pirate in the water tied it around Jack who fought against the restraints, but it was no use.

Jack scanned the area, unable to see any trace of his father. "Dad? Dad? Help me!"

"Looking for yer Dad are ye?" the captain leered from the deck of his ship. "I called Occy to feed jus' now and she didn't come. I guess she already ate." The captain roared with laughter and he was soon joined by the other pirates on the deck.

Jack inhaled sharply. So he *had* seen a monster in that cave, and his dad had supposedly been its lunchtime snack. How was all this possible? His eyes stung with tears. *Please don't let any of this be real. Pirates, mermaids, and a giant octopus. I must be dreaming.*

Jack was pulled up onto deck by the rope and he glanced around at the sneering pirates circling him. Jack wrinkled his nose at the smell. It wasn't body odour, but a mixture of fresh and stale farts. His stomach spasmed and he dry-retched.

The pirate who pulled him out of the water handed the boot to the captain. "Yer boot, cap'n." He bowed, and with a flourish, handed the captain the boot.

The captain took it and shifted his weight to the side, letting rip. The pirate standing next to him crinkled his nose and took a small sidestep away.

The name explained, Jack looked up at the pirate. He already wore one boot, and his other leg ended in a stump of wood. "Why do you need the boot, Captain Gas Pants?" Jack asked.

"It's pronounced, Gar-Puntz," the captain growled. "The 's' is silent." He glared at a few of the pirates who quickly stopped snickering.

The parrot squawked on the captain's shoulder. "Craaawk. Kill the kid. Kill the kid. Crawwwwk."

The captain chuckled and patted his bird. "Not just yet, Crackers." He tore off the sole of his shoe to reveal a secret waterproof compartment. He pulled out a roll of fabric that when laid out before him, revealed a map to buried treasure. A large red 'X' was painted in one corner, while the rest of the map was marked with land lines and weird symbols.

"Argh, thank the mighty sea Kraken that ye didn't steal me map." The captain turned to his crew. "Coz what do we do to thieves?" His shouts barely masked another fart.

"We cut off their hands!" they cheered, plugging their noses.

"But, but I didn't steal anything. I was fishing and my line caught your boot." Jack glanced around nervously.

The captain scratched his beard. "I know you didn't steal anything, m'boy. But me last deckhand did."

A lump of a young boy stepped forward. He was covered in dirt, scars and blisters. He held two stumpy arms out in front of him.

"We caught him stealing from the treasure room so we chopped off both his hands. But now he's useless t'us. Who's gonna cook our meals? Scrub our floors? Clean our toilets? Cut my toenails?" The captain farted again.

Jack held back the bile that threatened to spew forth.

"But, my family. I have friends, and school."

The captain threw an arm around Jack. "We're your family now. No need fer an edumacation when yer a pirate!"

As a bucket and scrubbing brush was shoved into Jack's hands, the crew burst into a rendition of a horribly tuned sea shanty.

When Drop Bears Attack

"In a few minutes we'll be stopping at the Cullawine National Park. You'll have an hour to explore the area, before returning to the bus for the included lunch. If you have any questions, fire away and I'll do my best to answer them." Gazza, the tour guide, scratched his bushy beard and adjusted his khaki shorts and shirt. "Cullawine National Park was founded in..."

Jessica stared out the window and allowed the tour guide's voice to wash over her. She didn't much care for the park itself or the history behind anything. The only thing she cared about today was cuddling a koala bear. And keeping cool. Jessica wiped her forehead and adjusted the fan vents to blow full bore directly on her. She hadn't expected the Australian summer to be that much hotter than a British one. Boy, was she wrong.

Towering eucalyptus trees flew by the windows in a blur as the small bus travelled down the dusty highway. It slowed and made a screeching right turn, leaving the smooth sealed road behind to bump and vibrate along the new dirt one. A big sign post read: 'Welcome to Cullawine National Park. Please take your litter with you.'

"So that's everything you need to know about the park and its history. After lunch, I'll take you into the koala sanctuary where you can all cuddle and get your included photo with a koala!"

Cheers erupted from the other tourists on board. Jessica took a moment to glance around. The bus was half full. There was Jessica, her mum, and grandparents, a lady journalist behind them jotting things down on a notepad, a middle-aged Italian couple up front, and an American couple at the back with their older teenage son.

"Once you've had enough of the koalas, there's a small zoo you can check out with other Australian critters such as kangaroos, wallabies, emus, dingoes, and a few snakes."

Jessica felt her mum stiffen at the mention of snakes. She sniggered, imagining her mum coming face to face with a massive Australian python. Snakes didn't bother Jessica, and she hoped she'd be able to touch one later, and maybe even scare her mum with it.

"Mum, doesn't Australia have the most poisonous snake in the world?"

Gazza glanced over at Jessica, a few rows from the front, and grinned. "Technically, the most venomous snake is a sea snake, but we have most of the other lethally venomous snakes in our backyard. But don't you worry, there is nothing at Cullawine National Park that can kill you." He paused, and bit his bottom lip. He looked side to side with a concerned look on his face. "Just, watch out for those drop bears."

"Give me a break. Drop bears aren't real," the American teen called out from the backseat.

Murmuring started throughout the bus. Everyone seemed to have an opinion on the drop bears. Jessica had heard from her friend Samantha that drop bears were a joke that Australians play on tourists. Samantha flew out to Australia every second year to visit her aunt and uncle, so she knew what she was talking about. Gazza was just trying to be entertaining.

"Oh no, m'boy. You've got that wrong." Gazza paused to stare out the window as the bus slowed to a stop in an otherwise empty car park. "Let's all get off the bus and I'll tell you everything I know about drop bears."

The Italians were the first off the bus and everyone followed them, crowding around Gazza as he began to tell his tale.

"The drop bear, or Thylarctos Plummetus, is found in forests just like this." He paused for effect, waving his hand to indicate the eucalyptus trees around them. In a matter-of-fact voice, Gazza continued, "They can grow to the size of a teenager, and can weigh up to 120 kilograms. Drop bears are carnivorous, unlike their herbivore koala cousins. They hide up in trees and ambush their victims as they walk underneath. They can drop from a height of eight meters uninjured. They have large, sharp teeth that they use to eat their prey. Sometimes, they'll drag their meal up a tree to feast on later."

Jessica knew it was a hoax, but the way Gazza told the story did make her wonder if there was any truth to his words. A shiver ran down her spine and she glanced up at the trees nervously.

"I hope you all ate Vegemite for breakfast this morning." He scanned the group, his face falling in horror. "No? No one?" He wiped his face with his hand, then chewed on a knuckle. "Vegemite is the only thing that repels them. No one read the brochure?"

"Good story, Gazza," snorted the teenage American. He plugged in his earphones. "That story might make today bearable."

Gazza chuckled at the pun, but then his face turned serious. "It's no joke, Paul." He pulled up his shirt to show glossy white scars running down his side from his chest to his hip. The skin was mottled with pink blotches. His voice came out as barely a whisper. "No joke."

Paul froze and pulled his earphones out. "What happened to you?"

"I survived a drop bear attack."

The Italians started speaking in rapid-fire Italian, gesturing their hands at the scar and then the trees and then each other.

Paul gave an awkward laugh. "Seriously though, what happened?"

Gazza shrugged his shoulders. "Drop bears."

Paul shook his head and rolled his eyes. He followed his parents off to the gift shop, putting his earphones back on.

Gazza shot Jessica a wink and a cheeky grin. Jessica didn't know what to think. She had thought it was all a joke up until he showed them his scars. It couldn't really have been a drop bear could it? It must have been from something else.

"Ah Gazza, before you head off, can I ask you those questions for my article?" the reporter asked.

"Course! I just gotta chuck a leak then I'll be right with you." He trotted off to the toilet and the reporter filed through the papers she was holding.

"We're burning daylight. Come on you lot." Jessica's Grandma traipsed over to the edge of the forest where a dirt path led them into the lush vegetation. Rocks and bushes covered the forest floor. A few fallen trees provided homes to small animals. Occasionally, a bush would rustle or Jessica would hear a slither or a scurrying of tiny feet. Hundreds of thick eucalyptus trunks grew out of the ground and reached up to the sky. Their leaves formed a thin canopy above them, allowing a speckling of sunlight to stream through the cracks.

Funnily enough, it was slightly cooler outside than it was on the bus thanks to a gentle breeze that rustled the trees. Out of the stuffy confines of the small vehicle, Jessica inhaled the clean country air, and swallowed a mouthful of dust. She took a sip from her bottle and nearly gagged on the warm water inside. Flies tried to drink the fluids from her eyes. She shooed them away, but they returned seconds later.

Jessica and her family followed the path a short while until they reached a fork in the road. A sign post offered two options. To the left was the easy trail. It was a gentle, twenty minute stroll through the forest. The trail to the right was marked as being more physically intense. A forty minute round trip would take them to a viewing deck that would give them a great view of a waterfall.

"I wouldn't mind seeing the waterfall," Jessica's Mum said, "But do you two think you'll be okay on the trail?" She eyed her parents.

"No matter what you think of us, we aren't invalids yet!" Jessica's Grandma replied with a huff. "If you bothered to spend more time with me, you'd know that I go on a hike a month with the club."

Jessica's Mum inhaled sharply. "Mum, I'm sorry. I didn't mean-"

"I know what you meant, I'm only teasing." Her Grandma smiled, but her eyes remained cold. "Come on Arthur, let's show these young ones that we're not old farts."

Jessica glanced up at her Mum who rolled her eyes. "You can't tell me off for rolling my eyes at you if you do it to your parents."

"Oh, God. Please don't tell me I annoy you as much as they annoy me?"

Jessica gave her mum a warm hug. "Never. I love you."

"I love you, too. I need to record you saying that so I can repeat it back to you in a few years when you hate me."

"I'll never hate you, Mum."

"I know, sweetie. Now come on, we better catch up or we'll never hear the end of it."

Jessica was glad her Mum had told her to change her shoes before they left. She had planned on wearing her sandals because she wanted to look good for the photo with the koala. But her mum had insisted she change into her hiking shoes and they had fought for several minutes before Jess gave in. The trail was covered in loose gravel and Jess slipped a handful of times. Without her sturdy shoes, she might have twisted her ankle. And looking good for the photo was already way out of the question. She was sweaty and covered in red dirt. *How do Australians live like this?*

The hike was easy enough to begin, but it wasn't long until it became demanding. Add the sticky heat and the flies that wouldn't stop bothering them, and Jessica was ready to return to the hotel and dive into the icy cold pool.

The trail led up an incline and Jessica's leg muscles burned from the exertion. The roar of the waterfall rumbled in the distance. The air grew more humid, and Jessica wiped her forehead several times. The trail eventually wound down to a wooden deck that opened up over the top of a waterfall.

Jessica leant against the railing and caught her breath. Her Grandma wasn't even slightly puffy, but her Grandpa was taking in steady breaths. She tried to breathe quietly and slowly, like she wasn't out of breath, but her lungs needed oxygen, stat! She coughed, using that as an excuse to loudly gulp in lungfuls of air.

She turned around and saw her mum had the camera out. "Okay, everyone, smile!"

The camera flashed and Jessica blinked away the black dots in her vision.

Over the sound of the waterfall, they heard voices carried on the wind. The Italians rounded the bend at a run.

"Oh good, I can ask them to take a photo of the four of us."

In between breaths, the man said, "Droppa bear!" He pointed behind him and jogged to them on the platform.

Jessica's Mum shook her head. "No. It's a joke. Joko?"

The Italian couple looked at her like she was crazy. She turned to her parents. "Bollocks. What's the Italian word for joke?"

"Scherzo," Jessica's Grandpa replied.

The Italian couple shook their heads furiously. "Essistono!"

Sighing, Jessica's mum handed them her camera, using hand signals to help get her message across. "You take photo of us and waterfall?"

They looked at the camera, then at each other, then bolted back the way they came, taking the camera with them.

"Seriously?" Jessica's mum charged after them.

Jessica glanced back at her grandparents who shooed her away. She raced after the stolen camera. Panting hard, she caught up to her mum who was right on the heels of the Italians.

They stopped in the middle of the trail and pointed to a shallow pothole in the path. Turning their heads towards the sky, the husband held the camera up, scanning the canopy.

"Idioto!" Her mum said. "Give me back my camera." She tried to take it out of his hands but he pushed her away.

A loud whooshing noise, followed by a thud sounded from somewhere back behind them, closer to the waterfall. Then another. Whoosh! Thud. Then a scream.

The Italians startled and spun with the camera up. "Droppa Bear. It attacka your familia."

Jessica's mum hesitated. "But there's no such thing as drop bears." It sounded more like a question than a statement.

Jessica turned and ran back to the waterfall. The noises did sound like something big and heavy dropping down onto the ground. She made it all the way back to the wooden lookout but couldn't see her grandparents anywhere. "Grandma? Grandpa?" she called, panic rising in her chest.

She ran back to her mum, stopping about half way because something shiny caught her attention. She bent down and picked up her grandma's glasses.

A crack sounded from one of the branches above her.

Jessica's gaze whipped upwards.

A flash of movement jumped from one tree to the next.

They were too high up, she couldn't see anything.

Something fell from the tree, something large. Jessica was just about to run when she saw what it was.

Her Grandpa's cardigan.

She picked it up and held it out in front of her. Half the material was shredded and there was something sticky on it. Jessica screamed when she realised it was blood. She dropped the cardigan and ran back to her mum.

She spotted her mum up ahead and ran into her, nearly bowling her over. "Drop bear! Ate Grandma and Grandpa! Run!"Jessica pulled on her mum's hand, but she remained rooted to the spot.

"Jessica, what's going on? Where are your grandparents?"

"Dead!" Jessica screamed, before bursting into tears. "They're gone. Drop bears pulled them up into the trees and ate them."

Her mum bit her lip then pulled her daughter into a hug. "Come on, I'm sure that's not what happened. Gazza's wild stories have put ideas into your head. They probably went off the trail to look at wildflowers or something. You know what they're like."

"Mum, I want to go back to the bus. Now." Jessica pushed herself out of her mum's embrace and started running back to the start of the trail. Her mum and the Italians followed close behind.

Her shoes crunched against the gravel on the trail as she sprinted along the path. Branches whipped past her face. Once or twice she almost stumbled on some loose rocks or a stray branch crossing the road.

Whoosh! Thud.

The Italian man screamed, his voice growing distant as if he were being pulled up into a tree.

Jessica pushed herself to run faster.

Whoosh! Thud.

The Italian woman shrieked, her voice getting fainter, just like her husband's.

The end of the trail was in sight. Jessica could see the trees parting and sunlight peeking through the loosely packed leaves. She pushed herself to run faster than she'd ever run before, despite her lungs and muscles protesting.

She saw the post that directed the two different paths and the bus that would provide her and her mum safety.

Whoosh! Thud.

A drop bear landed right in front of her.

The bear was a little taller than she was and beefed up like a rugby player. Fangs extended down from its top jaw, glistening with blood like the rest of its maw. Bloodshot eyes tracked Jessica's every movement. It coiled back onto its hind legs and pounced.

Jessica skidded to a stop and her mum pulled up beside her, placing a protective hand on Jessica's shoulder.

Another bear landed behind them and the ground trembled slightly.

Powerful arms pushed her out of harm's way. Jessica landed on the gravel and slid a metre into the bushes off the side of the track.

She watched the scene unfold in front of her in horror. Gazza must have heard her scream because he had appeared out of nowhere and was fighting the bears. One of the bears had her mum in its claws. Her mum screamed, punched, and kicked, but it was no use. The bear held on tightly.

Gazza had a knife that he was trying to stab the bear with. Every now and again he'd twist and slash at the bear behind him.

His knife struck the arm of the bear holding her mum and it let her go. She fell to her knees and crawled over to the bushes where Jessica cowered. "Come on, to the bus!" She helped Jessica stand and together they ran.

Gazza fought the two bears, his knife flashing in the midday sun as it sliced and stabbed at them. One of the bear's heads snapped around to track Jessica as she sprinted past, those yellow, bloodshot eyes following her. It pounced at her and latched onto her ankle.

Jessica went down and bit her tongue. A metallic taste filled her mouth and an explosion of pain erupted around her ankle. She kicked and thrashed, but the bear held on. It dragged Jessica backwards before it threw her over its shoulder and started climbing one of the tall eucalypts.

Gazza came flying out of nowhere and landed on its back, pulling it down to the ground. "Run! To the bus. Call for help!"

The drop bear let go of her ankle and Jessica jumped up and hobbled to safety, grunting with every burst of pain as she put weight on her sore leg.

Gazza's yells cut off suddenly.

She careened out of the bushes and into the sunlight. She didn't stop running until she reached the bus. Her mum caught up to her a few seconds later.

"Did Gazza...?" Her mum's voice trailed off.

"Get in the bus!" Jessica screamed at her mum and the reporter.

The reporter sat in her seat and sighed. "I'm starving. I hope lunch will be ready soon."

The Americans strolled back onto the bus as Jessica's mum attempted to use the radio to call for help and Jessica caught her breath.

"Where's Gazza?" the reporter asked. "He should be back with lunch by now."

From the edge of the bushes came an army of hungry drop bears. The reporter screamed and the Americans froze in their seats, mouths and eyes wide open. Jessica's mum latched the bus door shut as they raced forwards. They crashed into the bus, rocking it wildly to the side.

"Come on. Where are they?" Jessica's fingers shook madly while she and her mum desperately searched for a set of keys to the bus. Jessica punched a padded seat when they came up empty.

The drop bears continued to pound the bus. One of the windows fractured, but held.

Smash. Smash. Smash.

The cracks deepened, rippling out from the centre point until...

The window shattered and the drop bears poured into the bus.

They made short work of the people inside. Jessica kept a hand over her mouth and hid underneath one of the seats. Her breaths were stuttered and tears rolled down her face.

She squeezed her eyes shut and kept them shut, praying that everything would be okay.

In her panic, Jessica realised why no one believed in drop bears: they never left any survivors.

With a wrenching sound, the seat was pulled away from her and flung out of a window with an explosion of glass. Jessica cried out and opened her eyes.

A glob of drool landed on her shoulder. She barely had the opportunity to suck in enough air for a scream before the drop bear descended on her.

Oliver's Rosy Attitude

Oliver's fingers furiously worked the buttons on his game controller. "Die zombies, die!"

His onscreen character stood before a tidal wave of moaning zombies. They poured into the room from the doors, windows, ceiling, and any crack or crevice they could find. Oliver's gun ran out of ammo. Without missing a beat, he pressed a button and brought up a new, fully loaded weapon. "You're not going to beat me this time."

"Oliver! Put that flaming game down and get out here now!" Oliver's dad called from outside.

"I can't. Give me two more seconds. I've almost passed the level!"

The back door slid open and his Dad's head poked around the corner. "You said that fifteen minutes ago. Turn it off, now."

Oliver sat on the edge of the couch, feet tapping in excitement. His character still had full health, and the horde of zombies was quickly thinning out. This was it, he was about to pass the most difficult level in the game and unlock the bonus map! Oliver grinned as he gunned down the last remaining zombies.

Oliver's dad walked up to the television and pulled the plug out of the wall.

The screen went black.

"What did you do that for?" Oliver threw down the controller in a rage.

"I asked you nicely and gave you plenty of warning. This is your own fault." Oliver's dad stood there with a smug grin on his face, twirling the power cord in his hand. "As soon as the garden's done, you can come back in and play."

"But I have homework to do. I can't help you with the gardening right now." Oliver crossed his arms and huffed. Five more seconds. That's all that he needed to finish the level and save his progress.

His dad lowered his eyes. "Really? Well, if you've got homework, no more games for the rest of the day. You can help me in the garden then get onto your studies."

Oliver scowled. "Fine, I'll help you." He stood up and followed his dad outside. "Only because I have to," he added under his breath.

Snatching the plastic bag out of his dad's hands, Oliver walked around the garden, violently ripping out weeds from the garden bed. He muttered to himself as he yanked out weed after weed. "Slave labour. Dad wanted this stupid house. Not me. Why am I stuck out here working? I didn't want to move so I shouldn't be doing all the work. If I can't pass that level when I get back inside, Dad will pay."

"I can hear you, you know?" Oliver's dad put down the pruning shears and removed his gloves. The hedge he was trimming was half neat and angular, and half a wild mess. "I know you didn't want to move, but we couldn't afford to stay at the old place anymore. The rent was too expensive." He stepped back to admire the house. "I still can't believe our luck at finding a place like this so cheap. The previous owners, whatever happened to them, won awards for this garden. I'm sure we could have it looking amazing in no time. Sure, it needs a lot of work, but a bit of gardening never killed anyone, right?"

The hedge's leaves behind his dad rustled in the breeze, as if they were laughing at him.

Oliver let out a long sigh. "I know. I'm sorry. But I was so close to finishing that game. Why did you have to cut the power? I've been trying to pass that level for weeks and I was so close."

Oliver's dad slid his hands back into his gloves. "I'm sorry for pulling the plug on your game, but I just want you to listen and help out a bit more. You haven't bothered to help your mother or I for months. If you can't stop being so selfish and lazy, the PlayStation is going in the bin." He picked up his tools and returned to the hedge before Oliver could argue back.

Oliver stood there breathing heavily. A thousand arguments rose to the surface. His muscles twitched with anger, and as much as he wanted to explode, he knew the right thing to do was keep his mouth shut and keep his parents happy. If he could give them what they wanted, they'd hopefully leave him alone to play his game.

The sun warmed Oliver's back as he filled three more garbage bags with weeds. After what felt like an eternity, but a quick check of his watch showed it had only been forty minutes, Oliver stood and stretched. He wiped the sweat from his forehead. He had vanquished the invading weed army.

Swallowing his frustration and feeling exhausted, Oliver mustered all the happiness he could gather. "I've finished with the weeds. Can I go back inside now?"

A few snips of the pruning shears later, and Oliver's dad had finished shaping the hedges into a geometric green wall. "Before you go inside, let me show you how to use the lawnmower."

Oliver clenched his jaw and bit back a retort. "Fine."

The lawnmower sputtered to life as Oliver's dad pulled the cord to start the engine. Oliver pushed the mower up and down the lawn in rows, culling the thick green blades down to short stumps. He looked over at his father who walked past the rose bushes along the side fence to the veggie garden in the corner. The roses almost seemed to follow Oliver's dad as he walked past.

Oliver killed the lawnmower's engine and turned to admire his work. The grass had clearly been cut by an amateur, patches of longer grass poked up among the sections that had been cut properly, but at least it was cut. His father should be happy with that much.

His dad glanced up. "You all done?" He removed his gloves and rubbed his chin. "Seriously? Come on, take some pride in your work."

"Can you show me?" Oliver asked. He stepped aside as his father took over, finishing up the lawn in a fraction of the time it would have taken Oliver. Pleased with himself for tricking his dad into finishing the job, Oliver made an obvious effort of looking around the garden. "Looks good now. We've done a great job. Do you want me to get you a drink on my way inside?"

"The more you try and fight me, the longer I'll keep you out here. Help me with the rose bushes." His dad showed Oliver how and where to trim the roses back. "Be careful of the thorns, they're sharp."

The roses almost seemed to shrink back, as Oliver and his dad removed the dead canes with their secateurs. Together, they worked in silence. A cloud passed over the sun, making the world seem dark for a few moments, before the light returned.

After they finished, the roses almost appeared to sigh in appreciation. They were impressive, the roses. There were a dozen of them in a line. Most of the flowers were blood red, but there were a few whites and yellows and one pink variety as well.

Oliver removed his gloves and threw them to the ground. "I'm beat," he said.

"You're actually doing a really good job." Oliver's dad clapped him on the shoulder.

Oliver's chest swelled with pride. "Thanks, Dad." He wouldn't admit it, but the more he worked with his dad, the more he enjoyed it. But not as much as playing his game.

"How about you pick one of the roses and take it inside for Mum?"

Oliver nodded and chose the largest red rose. He reached towards it but it moved slightly, and his finger caught the thorn instead of the bare stalk he had aimed for. He inhaled sharply at the sting. He tried to get a hold of the flower three more times, but every time he reached for it, a thorn would prick his finger. He pulled back his hand and shook it several times before stopping to examine the small but growing beads of blood. This battle wound would provide him with an honourable discharge from further gardening service.

He showed his hand to his father. "You said gardening won't kill me, but it's dangerous to my health, look."

His dad winced. "Only you could end up with a handful of cuts from a rose bush." He shook his head. "Leave the flower for me, go inside and get cleaned up."

Oliver jogged inside. The weed rebels had been taken care of and his duty was over.

"I've still got a few jobs left to do. As soon as you're finished in there come back out," his dad called after him.

Oliver sighed. His commander was tough.

Humming came from the kitchen, and Oliver found his mum unpacking boxes of crockery and cutlery into their drawers and cupboards. She glanced up as Oliver walked in. "Oh honey, what's wrong?"

"I got a few cuts from the rose bush, and they won't stop bleeding." Oliver stuck out his hand for his mum to see.

"Quick, put it under some running water to clean it out. I'll go get the first aid kit." She hustled out of the room, returning a few seconds later with the red case.

Oliver turned on the tap and examined his hand. The skin around the wounds was hard and brown, it felt like a splinter was stuck in there, and the area around it was red. It had finally stopped bleeding though.

His mum dabbed the cuts with antiseptic, and Oliver rocked on the balls of his feet, grimacing.

"Let's see if I can get these splinters out." She wrapped her hand around his and took a pair of tweezers to his fingers.

After several minutes of painful digging around in the cuts, his mum gave up. "This is useless. Honey, I'm sorry. I'll give you some Band-Aids and give those splinters some time to work their way out on their own."

"Sure, thanks, Mum. Can I go back outside and help dad now? He *really* needs my help and even though the pain is *excruciating*, I want to help him finish."

"No, you've done enough. I'll tell him you've hurt your hand." She patted his hand.

It took all of Oliver's will power to not jump for joy. He fought the grin spreading across his face with an overcompensated frown. "I wanted to go back out and help, but my hand is just too sore." He sighed. "I guess there's not much I can do, but sit down and play my game."

Putting the plug back in the wall, Oliver switched on the console and jumped on the couch. The game loaded and he worked his way back to the impossible level, wincing and grimacing every time he put pressure on his cuts.

Thanks to his sore hand, Oliver didn't play as well as he had earlier that day. The more he played, the more his fingers throbbed and the angrier he got. After dying for the fifth time in a row, Oliver dropped the controller and balled his fists in anger. He was so frustrated it seemed like the ground was trembling.

"Oliver!" his dad called from outside. His voice was loud, and did he sound scared?

Peering through the window, Oliver's jaw hung open at the sight of his father standing in the middle of the lawn being attacked by the roses. He swung his shears left, right and centre at the rose bushes that ran around him on their wiry roots for legs. They dodged his swings and lashed out with their branches. Oliver watched in horror as they shepherded him back towards the grape vine growing along the back wall next to the hedge.

Oliver ran outside, calling out for his mum as he bolted to his father. He stopped in his tracks as the grape vines whipped out and wrapped themselves around his dad's arms and legs. A scream was cut off as a bunch of grapes was shoved into his mouth. The grape vines held him in place as the rose bushes cut and swiped and stabbed him with their thorns.

Oliver's stomach rolled over as his dad's body shrivelled and shrunk, his skin turning a coarse brown. His hair and fingers lengthened into bushy bunches of green leaves. His feet elongated into long roots that penetrated the ground. He tilted his head back and Oliver got one last look at his father before he completely turned into a rose bush himself. His eyes were the last things to change. They popped out of his head and stretched out, turning into two red rose buds.

"What's your father up to out there?" Oliver's mum asked as she stepped out beside Oliver. She peered out over the garden and lifted a hand to her mouth. "What's gotten into him? He's ripped up all the beautiful roses!"

Oliver didn't answer. He barely registered his mum standing right next to him. Pressure built up where the cuts on his fingers were. The bandage had puffed up, as if there was heaps of padding on his finger. After seeing what had happened to his dad, it could only mean one thing.

He ripped the bandages off and saw what he was afraid of. Leaves sprouted from his fingers.

Oliver's mum barged out into the middle of the lawn. "Oliver, come here and help me. The roots look intact; I think if we replant them straight away they might survive." She lovingly picked up one of the rose bushes and took it over to the garden bed where it came from. "Peter! Where are you? What on Earth were you thinking?"

Oliver tore his eyes away from his hand and saw his mum near the roses. "No mum! Get away from them!"

His mother shrieked as the rose bush in her hands started thrashing wildly, cutting her skin with its thorny limbs. She fell backwards and the other roses jumped on her in a pile. Her screams died as her body transformed into a smaller rose bush with white flowers.

The roses turned their attention to Oliver and he realised the danger he was in. He didn't want to end up a rose bush like the rest of his family. But looking down at his hand, maybe it was too late?

He turned to run away, but blades of grass lengthened and wrapped around his ankle. Oliver fell flat on his stomach.

Before he could get up, the rose bushes attacked. Sharp stabs of pain lanced across his body as he screamed and writhed in place.

The garden grew bigger.

No. He grew smaller.

His toes lengthened into long roots that dove into the soft ground. Water drew up from his toes and flowed through his body. He tasted dirt. Thorns sprung up across his skin, ripping his clothes to shreds. Leaves budded on his arms, legs, and torso, extending outwards as they unfurled.

The pain dulled, his movements slowed and he looked upon the world through his rose-tinted vision.

Oliver followed the other roses back to the garden bed along the side of the house, taking his place between his mother and father.

He had nothing to do but grow and bloom and grow some more. And when the next family moved in, he would welcome his new brothers and sisters.

A Moonlit Date

A light knock sounded at the front door, rudely interrupting Noah from his reading.

"Can someone get that for me, please?" Noah's Mum yelled from her bathroom. She had been in there for over an hour already getting ready for another dumb date with Steve. Ugh.

Noah sighed and dragged his feet to the front entrance. He put on a scowl and opened the door.

Steve stood under the porch light wearing a pair of neat black pants and an open-neck baby blue shirt, a bright grin plastered on his stupid face. He had dark brown hair, with patches of grey along the sides. Noah's mum called Steve hirsute, but that was just a fancy way of saying he was hairy. "It makes him seem more manly," his mum would say.

"Hey, Noah! How was school today?" Steve asked.

Noah shrugged. "Fine."

"Mind if I come in?"

Noah contemplated making him wait outside, or telling him that his mum wasn't here, but then thought better of it. His mum would probably end up grounding him if he did. Noah stepped aside and allowed Steve to pass.

"Mum's in the bathroom. Hopefully she won't be too much longer." Noah closed the front door.

"That's fine, I don't mind waiting." Steve traipsed through the house to the living room.

Yeah, but I do! Noah thought to himself.

Emily came downstairs. "Hey, Steve." She waved.

"Hi, Emily. Are you babysitting Noah tonight?" Steve plopped himself down on their dad's leather armchair.

Noah balled his fists at his side. No one was allowed to sit on his dad's chair. *Who does Steve think he is? Sitting in Dad's chair and calling me a baby?* "I don't need a babysitter," Noah growled.

Steve threw his hands in the air. "I'm sorry, I didn't mean babysitter, I just meant-"

"Yes, I'm *babysitting* you, aren't I?" Emily cooed, walking over to Noah and ruffling his hair.

Noah shrugged her off and she trotted over to the kitchen where she pulled out a jug of water from the fridge. "Can I get you a drink?" she asked.

"No, I'm okay, thanks." Steve scratched behind his ear and his right leg twitched a little bit.

"I'll have a glass, thanks." Noah sat on the couch opposite Steve and glared at him before returning to his book.

Emily poured one glass of water then put the jug back. She drained the glass and then put it in the sink.

"Hey, I asked for a glass of water!"

"If you want one, you can get it yourself." She poked her tongue out at Noah and ran upstairs.

How could Noah enjoy his book with Steve sitting in his dad's chair? Every few words, Noah peered over the top of his book to glare at Steve. *Hurry up Mum!*

Steve leaned forwards in the chair. "So, Noah, I've got two tickets for the footy this weekend. Do you wanna come and watch it with me?"

Noah sighed and put his book down. Couldn't Steve see that he was busy and didn't want to talk? If he wanted to talk he wouldn't have picked up the book. He thought he made it very clear.

"Sounds like fun, Steve. Thanks for the offer, but I'm busy." It didn't sound like fun. It sounded like torture. The only thing that Noah hated more than watching sport was playing it. He was skinny and uncoordinated so he usually ended up embarrassing himself when he played. And he hated that Steve was trying to replace his own father. He didn't need another one. He ground his teeth. His dad was going to come back. Why didn't anyone else believe him?

"That's a shame." For a brief moment, Steve looked relieved.

"Oh, wait," Noah said. *If Steve doesn't really want to take me, maybe I will go?* "Did you say this weekend? Actually, I think I'm free. Let's go."

Steve's lips twitched into a tight smile. "Excellent."

Inside his head, Noah danced his happy dance. He didn't know how yet, but somehow he was going to use that game to sabotage Steve's new relationship with his mum.

At that moment, his mum's high heels clicked down the hall and she entered the room. "Oh, hi Steve. Can you please give me a hand with my dress?"

Noah groaned. He hated it when his mum made herself look so pretty. She was his mum. She shouldn't look nice, she should just look normal.

Steve leapt off the couch and zipped up the back of her purple dress. "You look stunning."

She gave Steve a peck on the lips and Noah gagged.

"What have you got planned for tonight?" She asked, clasping a pearl necklace around her neck.

"Well, I've got a pack of mates that have just opened a new restaurant around the corner and they serve a really good steak. It's a nice night; I thought we could walk there and back under the full moon through the park."

She clapped her hands and held them up to her mouth. "That sounds perfect, and so romantic. Let me grab my coat."

Noah glowered at Steve who winked at him. He picked up his book and started reading again.

"Okay, bye sweetie." She kissed Noah's forehead and held Steve's hand by the front door. "I'm going to lock the door, okay? Stay inside and don't open it for anyone."

"Yes, Mum. Now can I finally get back to my book?"

"Of course. Love you. Bye." The door closed and was followed by the clicking of two locks.

Emily came downstairs. "Have they gone? Good. Try not to burn the house down or anything, okay?"

"Ha ha, very funny." Noah scrunched up his face and went cross-eyed.

"And *that's* why you still need a babysitter. Real mature." Emily turned and headed upstairs.

"What are you doing?"

She paused near the top of the stairs. "I'm calling Dean. If you interrupt me I'll tell mum you opened the door for a stranger," she said before disappearing from sight.

Noah groaned and picked up his book. He didn't understand why both his mum and sister had such bad taste in men. He returned to his story about a kid at school who got bitten by a wolf one day. A few days later, under the full moon, he turned into a werewolf. Noah was so close to finding out who the werewolf was that bit him. He eagerly read on.

He turned, page after page, until...

It was the maths teacher from school!

Noah slapped his thigh. He should have known! The book hinted at it earlier on, the guy was hairy and liked eating really rare steaks.

Noah dropped his book. Steve was hairy. And what did Steve say he was going to do with his mum? Take her out to a steak bar. And then a walk under the full moon. *Steve's a werewolf! And he's going to bite Mum!*

The more Noah thought about it, the more it made sense. Steve scratched his ear earlier just like a dog did. Maybe he had fleas? He loved ball sports and running. There was no denying it, he was a werewolf.

Noah raced upstairs and banged hard on Emily's locked door. "Emily! Emily! Emily! Mum's in danger!"

"I swear I'm going to kill you!" Emily screamed at Noah from inside her bedroom. There was a loud crash on the door from her side. She must have thrown something. "Leave me alone!"

"No, Emily, I'm serious. Mum's really in danger." He bounced on the balls of his feet.

"Sorry, Dean. I'll call you back in a minute. We're having a *Noah problem* again."

Noah didn't like the way Emily said 'Noah problem', but he didn't have time to fight with her. Their mum was in danger.

The lock clicked and Noah pushed the door open. "Steve's a werewolf!"

Emily's eyes bulged wide. "Really? Oh my gosh! We have to save Mum!" Her shocked expression cracked and she rolled her eyes. "You need to stop reading scary books if you're too young to know the difference between real and make believe."

"I'm twelve, Emily. And you're only two years older, so you can't boss me around." Noah folded his arms and tried to mimic the sassy expression on his sister's face.

Emily laughed at him. "Are you constipated? Now can you leave me alone so that I can get back to my conversation with Dean?"

"Emily, I'm serious. Steve's a werewolf. Think about it. He's taking mum for steak, he's hairy, he's obsessed with football, he runs a lot, he calls his friends 'his pack' and he said he wants to take mum for a walk under the full moon."

"He's pretty much perfect, isn't he?" She sighed. "Except for the hairy part. I'll make Dean shave if he gets too hairy when we're married." She shook herself out of her daydream. "Okay, are we done now?"

"You have to believe me! He's going to attack mum."

Emily rolled her eyes so far back Noah wondered if she saw her brain. Probably not. Just an empty space where a brain should be. "There is no such thing as werewolves, you doofus," Emily said.

"Well, I don't trust him so I'm going to follow them. If you let me leave the house on my own you'll get in big trouble. You know mum makes us stay indoors when it's a full moon. What if I bump into a crazy person? Crime rates are higher, too. I could get kidnapped or something and it'll be all your fault." Noah turned to leave but was stopped when Emily held onto his shoulder. She was stronger than she looked.

"Noah," she said softly. "If this is about Dad, you should drop it. You didn't know him like I did."

Tears formed in Noah' eyes. He squeezed them shut, hoping Emily didn't notice. He turned to face his sister. "This has nothing to do with dad." Deep down, he knew Emily was right, that it had everything to do with Dad. But that didn't mean he had to give up hope. It had been four years since their dad left. There was still a chance he would come back.

Emily sighed and pulled Noah into a hug. "Okay, if it will make you feel better, let's go for a walk. We'll check on Mum and Steve, realise that Mum's fine and Steve's not a werewolf, and come straight home." Emily pushed Noah away and stared into his eyes. "But you have to promise me you won't tell mum about this. It'll be our little secret. Deal?"

"Thanks!" Noah said, "You're the best!"

"I know." Emily playfully ruffled Noah's hair. "Just give me a minute, I have to tell Dean that I'll be gone for a while."

Noah went downstairs and found his coat. He stood at the front door for a minute, waiting for Emily, before he realised that he was soon going to be face to face with a werewolf and he had nothing to protect himself, Emily, or his mum.

He rifled through the drawers of the display cabinet that housed his grandma's fine china. His mum didn't really like the set, but it was the only thing she had left of her mum. He found what he was looking for and pulled out one of the silver knives.

He knelt down and put the handle inside his sock. The cool metal pressed against his skin and he felt like a monster hunter. He was going to be a hero!

Standing up slowly, he took a few steps and made sure that he wasn't going to accidentally stab himself with the knife.

"Hurry up, Emily!" He called from the front door.

"I'm coming, I'm coming," she said as she jogged down the stairs. "Are you all set?"

"Yep, let's go."

Emily locked the door behind her and they walked down the driveway and onto the footpath that would lead them to the park. The street lights illuminated the yards of their neighbours. All but one had neatly trimmed lawns and clear driveways. One house in the middle of the street had overgrown lawns and the owners never smiled or waved when they came or left.

Their world darkened as they left the street behind them and followed the footpath into the park. The night was overcast and didn't provide much light. Thick clouds hid the moon that would turn Steve into a monster. A playground sat off to their right with a half-pipe just behind that. To the left was a dense wooded area

The path wound around the edge of the trees. A rustling sound deep within the bushes made Noah pause. "Shh." He put a finger to his mouth. "Did you hear that?"

Emily stopped, cocking her head to the side. "Nothing."

Noah searched for the source of the noise but the trees were too thick and it was too dark to see anything beyond the first few rows. He sensed movement a little deeper in.

"I think there's someone in there."

Sighing, Emily pulled out her phone and switched on the flashlight app. She waved it in front of the trees. "See? Nothing." The light washed over their feet as she made to turn it off.

"Help!" a man's voice cried deep within the woods.

"Did you hear that?" Noah spun around to face his sister whose face was drained of colour.

"Was that…" Emily began, "Did that sound like Steve to you?"

"He's probably trying to lure us in there so he can attack us too. If he's in there, then so is Mum. We need to save her!" Noah ran towards the trees, but turned away quickly when heavy footsteps started running towards him.

"Help me!" Steve's panicked voice shouted.

A howl sounded even deeper in the woods, sending shivers running down Noah' spine.

Emily grabbed Noah's hand and her fingernails dug into his skin. "He's coming. Run!" She tried to drag Noah away, but he stood rooted to the spot.

Despite his hammering heart, Noah had a job to do. "No. We have to save mum."

Steve burst out of the woods, his shirt shredded and bloodied around his left shoulder which had the unmistakeable bite marks of a wolf. They were fresh. His eyes grew wild at the sight of the kids and he backpedalled. "Stay away from me. You and your freaky mum."

Noah pulled the silver knife from his sock and brandished it in front of him. "Stay away from me, werewolf!"

The clouds started to expose part of the moon, and a ray of moonlight shone down on Steve like a spotlight. Noah and Emily remained in the darkness, watching in horror as Steve's face contorted in pain and confusion as he rubbed the bite mark on his shoulder.

"What?" Steve barked. "I'm not a werewolf. It's your-"

A sound like a gunshot rang out and Steve dropped to all fours, with a yelp of pain. Steve writhed on the ground, screaming as his body popped, cracked, ripped and snapped itself into a half-human half-wolf form.

Course brown hairs erupted all over his body and his mid section widened. His mouth and nose grew longer, teeth lengthened and a tail grew out of his backside. What remained of his clothes ripped away as the transformation completed.

Noah turned to his sister who stood there shaking from head to toe. "See! I told you Steve is a werewolf." Then he rounded on Steve, swallowing the hard lump in his throat.

"Wh-what have you done to my mum?" He held the silver knife in front of him and Steve whined.

Noah scanned the area for a sign of his mum, his heart rate spiking in fear. Where was she? Was she safe? Had she been bitten too? Noah prayed she was okay.

Steve the werewolf jumped up on all four legs and lowered his head. Saliva dripped from his snarling jaw. There was a hunger in his eyes that wasn't human, and Noah's knees trembled.

Emily grabbed Noah's hand and pulled him back. "Yeah, he's a werewolf. And we're his dinner." They slowly backed away from Steve, not making any sudden movements.

More pops and cracks came from inside the woods as Steve stalked closer to Noah and Emily.

"No, Steve!" Their mum burst out of the woods, wrapping her coat around herself. Her other clothes were gone. She stood between Steve and her kids. "No." Her voice was low.

Steve whimpered and lay down. His long tongue lolled out to the side.

"Mum, what's going on?" Emily cried.

Their mum's voice was shrill. "What are you doing out here? I told you to stay at home. You've put yourselves in danger."

The clouds continued to part from the moon, the warm glow fighting the darkness around Noah's and Emily's feet.

"Mum, please tell us what's going on?" Noah begged. "Did he bite you?"

She glanced up at the moon. "Run. Run home now. Before the moonlight reaches you. I'll explain it all when we're safely indoors."

Steve growled.

"Run!" their mum screamed.

Noah held out his hand into the moonlight that was inches from their bodies. Dark brown hairs sprouted from the back of his hand and his fingernails lengthened to pointy tips. He retracted his hand into the shadows and stared in horror as his hand returned to normal. "Mum?"

The moonlight hit their bodies, and two more gunshot cracks rang out into the otherwise quiet night. Noah convulsed with pain and he sensed Emily doing the same next to him. For an agonising minute, his body snapped, cracked, and popped its way into his new shape.

As the pain subsided, Noah was welcomed to a new world. He could smell the school cafeteria which was miles from here. He could see as if it was the middle of the day. His muscles twitched with speed and strength he had never known before.

Their mum walked over to Steve and nuzzled her head into his neck. "I'm sorry you had to find out this way, I wanted to wait until you both were older."

Noah tried to speak, but all he could do was growl and whine.

Their mum transformed into a midnight black wolf before their eyes. Her transition was a lot faster and seemingly less painful than Noah's had been.

"Why do you think I never let you out of the house on a full moon?" Her voice echoed inside Noah' head. "Your father and I were both werewolves when we met. When we had kids, we weren't sure whether you would be human or werewolf. There was a rumour going around that if you hadn't turned by your eighteenth birthday, you wouldn't ever turn."

"How come I can hear your voice in my head?" Noah thought.

"It's how we communicate in our wolf form." She padded over to Noah and Emily, nestling her snout between theirs.

"And Dad?" Noah asked.

The voice that entered his head this time was full of sadness. "He was attacked by one of the rival packs on the other side of town. I'm so sorry."

Noah barely registered Emily's question after his mum's revelation.

"So, how come Steve is a werewolf too?" Emily asked.

Their mum's eyes sparkled. "Steve proposed to me tonight, and I said yes."

"She said she was a werewolf and I honestly didn't believe her," Steve began. "So I said, yes, she could bite me thinking it was a joke, and then she did, and now I'm here." He pawed the ground. "I was a bit scared at first, but now, I'm starting to think I like this."

"What now?" Emily asked.

Their mum turned her head up at the yellow moon and let out a long howl. "We don't hunt people, only other animals. Smell that?"

Noah sniffed the air. Saliva dripped from his mouth. A meaty, gamey scent drifted towards him from the woods.

"There's a kangaroo in there with our names on it." His mother turned and prowled into the cover of the trees.

Noah bounded past her, allowing the wolf part of his brain to take over.

Dinner with Family

"What can I get you?" The waitress stood next to Kelly, smiling patiently. Her name tag read 'Rachel' which sat just under the small logo on her shirt: Tantalus Cafe. Her wiry brown hair was pulled back in a tight ponytail, making her large forehead even more pronounced. Her eyes were slightly pink and her teeth were a brilliant white, slightly more pointed than the average set.

Kelly sighed as she read the menu. The steak, meat lover's pizza, and burger all sounded nice, but were bigger than she could ever eat. She wasn't that hungry so she settled for something from the kids menu.

"I'll have the nuggets and chips, thanks." Kelly handed the waitress her menu.

Of course." Rachel winked. "You're so adorable, you know that? I could just eat you up." She flashed a pearly grin before turning to Kelly's parents. "And what can I get you two?"

"I'll have the schnitzel, thanks," Kelly's dad said. "What meat is it?"

Rachel smirked. "Like I haven't heard that joke before." She rolled her eyes in a playful way. "You know exactly what type of meat it is."

"Pork?" he asked, eyebrows knitting together in confusion.

Rachel chuckled to herself. "Yes. Pork." She continued chuckling to herself as she wrote it down on the pad.

Kelly's dad turned to her mum. "You wanted the same, didn't you?"

She nodded. "Yes, that creamy mushroom sauce sounds divine."

"Is that all?" Rachel licked her lips and took the menus from Kelly's parents.

"All good, thanks," Kelly's dad replied.

"Won't be too long." Rachel sang, before she bounced away to the kitchen.

"She's a bit odd, don't you think?" Kelly's dad whispered to her mum.

Kelly's eyes followed Rachel as she disappeared through the swinging kitchen doors. The place was deserted, and while that might have been a bad omen, it was only 5:30pm, so it was still early for the dinner rush.

Tantalus Cafe wasn't Kelly's first choice for dinner. The restaurant was very basic, with twenty tables scattered about the room with white plastic tablecloths and no decorations on the walls apart from an obnoxious red banner announcing their grand opening two weeks ago. No music played to add ambience to the room. But Kelly enjoyed listening to the pots and pans crashing in the kitchen and the sizzle of meat cooking over a hot stove.

Kelly's dad had only chosen this restaurant because he's the biggest cheapskate Kelly knew. After visiting her Grandma in the nearby nursing home, they had returned to their car to find a discount coupon under the windscreen wiper for twenty-five percent off the total bill.

"It's quite handy having this restaurant so close to Hope Springs. The food's really cheap here, and if it's nice, we can visit your mum and have dinner on the way home more often," Kelly's mum said.

Kelly couldn't resist groaning. "Ugh, I hate it there. Everything smells funny and all the old people want to touch me and talk to me."

"You'll be like that one day too, sweetie. Plus, it's the right thing to do. Imagine if you were all alone and your family never visited you?"

"But isn't that why they stay in places like Hope Springs? So they're surrounded by people their own age and we don't have to visit them so often?"

Her dad snickered. He shrugged when Kelly's mum glared at him. "What? She's got a point."

"We were lucky to get her into Hope Springs in the first place. A lot of residents have passed away these last two weeks. It's quite sad actually. But, that's the circle of life."

The kitchen doors burst open and Rachel returned, juggling their three huge plates of food on her arms. Kelly's mouth watered at the smell of the deep fried goodness coming her way. She took a sip from her glass of Pepsi and waited for the food to be placed in front of her. Her stomach rumbled.

She ogled her mountain of nuggets and chips, there was no way she was going to get through it all, and this was a kid's meal. Her parent's plates were even bigger. The ends of the schnitzels hung over the sides of the plates with a huge pile of chips underneath. The creamy scent of the earthy mushroom sauce was overpowering.

"I hope you enjoy your meal." Rachel licked her lips before trotting back to the kitchen.

Kelly dipped a nugget into the pool of tomato sauce and took a bite. A small puff of steam escaped, and it burned the roof of her mouth a little, but it was one of the best nuggets she had ever had. It tasted different to the chicken nuggets she was used to, but Kelly couldn't put her finger on what made it so special. Kelly popped a crispy golden chip into her mouth. "Mmm..." She chewed for a moment, relishing the taste. Just the perfect amount of salt and fluffy on the inside too.

"This is really good," Kelly's mum said in between bites. Her eyes glazed over with happiness.

"And for the price… I'd be willing to visit mum every weekend." Kelly's dad shovelled a forkful of schnitzel into his mouth.

Much to Kelly's surprise, their plates were spotless by the time they finished. Kelly leant back in her chair, rubbing her uncomfortably full belly. "I shouldn't have eaten that last nugget, but it tasted so good."

"I know how you feel." Her dad let out a small burp and undid his belt buckle. "That feels better. That was the best schnitzel I've ever had. That pork was so juicy."

Kelly stood. "I'll be back in a minute, I've got to use the toilet." She walked to the back of the restaurant, her stomach protesting with each step. Once she'd finished, she made her way back to the table when the door chimed. Another family walked in, clutching the same coupon Kelly's dad had used. Rachel came out of the kitchen and threw Kelly a smile before greeting the new patrons in a cheerful voice. The kitchen doors continued to swing.

Kelly's eyes widened at the sight of a little hunched over old lady being wheeled through the kitchen by one of the nurses from Hope Springs. Her wispy white shawl covered her shoulders as she looked around the kitchen with a confused expression on her face. Kelly blinked several times. What was Beryl doing there?

Kelly's grandma had mentioned that there was a wide variety of activities on offer at the retirement home. One of the activities had been a cooking class, but Kelly had assumed that they would have used the kitchen at the home. Is that why the menu was so cheap? Were they getting cheap labour from Hope Springs?

Her parents were deeply engrossed in conversation. They wouldn't miss her for a few more minutes.

Curiosity got the better of her and Kelly slipped through the swinging doors, finding herself standing before an enormous L-shaped commercial kitchen. It was toasty, and a range of spices and smells comforted her. Something chocolaty was baking in the oven and even though Kelly was full, there would be room for dessert when she got back to the table.

She followed the direction she had seen Beryl be wheeled in, and stopped when she heard voices near the cooler room.

"This is the last one for the week," a sweet female voice said. "You'll have to wait until next week or people will start to get suspicious."

"But we need more, it takes several weeks to marinate the meat, otherwise it's chewy and tough," answered a male in a gruff voice. "We need to get more meat processing otherwise we'll have nothing to serve our customers when we get busy."

Kelly crouched low behind a countertop. What they were talking about. What sort of meat needs that long to marinate?

"Fine," said the woman sharply. "I'll bring over one more, but that's it."

"Excellent," the man replied.

Kelly held her breath as footsteps drew closer. Fortunately, they continued past her without a glance, and exited out a back door, leaving her alone in the kitchen.

She peered around the corner and saw Beryl slumped in her wheelchair in front of the cool room. Kelly tiptoed over to her and tapped her on the shoulder. "Beryl, it's Kelly. Do you remember me? Are you alright?"

Beryl whimpered. Her eyes shot open. "Help me!"

Kelly gasped and jumped backwards. "What's wrong?"

"They're going to eat me!"

Kelly sighed and crouched in front of Beryl, resting a hand on her knee. "It's okay. Do you know where you are? You're here for your cooking class." Kelly felt a pang of sadness for the old woman. Her mind was failing her which was a scary reality about the aging process. She had seen the same thing with her grandma. Some days, her grandma couldn't remember who Kelly was. She hated it.

Tears ran down Beryl's cheek and she shook her head.

The doorknob on the back door turned and Kelly panicked. She knew she shouldn't be in the kitchen and she didn't want to get caught. Glancing back at the restaurant, she realised she wouldn't make it in time. The only option was to hide in the freezer and wait until the kitchen emptied again so she could sneak out.

She wrenched open the cool room door and crept inside. Shivering, she wrapped her arms around herself after she closed the door behind her. Her breath misted in front of her eyes.

Footsteps crunched on the other side of the cool room, and Kelly scolded herself for her own stupidity. *Idiot! Now I'll be in even more trouble when they find me. I should have made a run for the restaurant.*

Metal shelves surrounded her loaded with containers of meat. Kelly glanced at a few containers. "Schnitzel" – Martin. 24th April. "Burger patties" – Alfred. 13th April. "Kebabs" – Elizabeth. 14th April. "Nuggets" – Roger. 21st April. *Why have they named their food? That seems a bit odd.*

Beryl's words echoed in Kelly's mind: 'They're going to eat me.' Kelly's stomach spasmed. "No," she breathed.

At that moment, the cool room doors flew open and Rachel stood there with Kelly's parents. "See, I told you we would find your daughter, she's just been exploring." Her voice was sing-songy, but her eyes were icy daggers that cut through Kelly. "What have you been doing, hon?"

A man wearing a greasy apron came into view behind her parents, a cleaver clutched in his pudgy hand. His thin lips twisted into a smirk, pointed teeth shining under the bright, artificial light. "How did you like the nuggets?" he grunted. "Were they to *die* for?"

Kelly whimpered and ran to her dad, hugging his side. "Can we get out of here, please? This place is scary!"

Beryl hung her head in her hands. "I tried to warn you," she moaned. "Now they're going to eat you too."

Rachel wiped a bit of drool from the corner of her mouth. "I didn't realise you weren't one of us."

"One of what?" Kelly's mum asked.

The chef sniffed the air with closed eyes. "I haven't had the opportunity to work with such *fresh* ingredients since our last restaurant near the orphanage got closed down by the authorities."

"What's going on here?" Kelly's dad crossed his arms and glared at the chef.

"We're going to be added to the menu," Kelly wailed. She didn't believe it though, she knew her dad would protect her and save them from this horrible place. Then they'd go to the police and save the old timers from Hope Springs.

"Not if I can help it." With surprising strength and speed, Beryl rammed her wheelchair into the chef and he stumbled onto the stove.

He yelled, dropping his cleaver and clutching his sizzling hands.

"Run!" Beryl cried, and Kelly didn't need to be told twice.

She ran for the restaurant, with her parents right behind her, but stopped short at the sight of the now full restaurant.

Half the tables were occupied, and the people sitting there all glanced up as Kelly burst through the swinging doors. As one, they licked their lips and ogled her with pink, hungry eyes.

From inside the kitchen, Rachel cried out. "Meals on wheels! Whoever catches them gets to eat them!"

A portly lady nearby leapt from the table. "I call dibs on the girl!"

The others scrambled from their seats, drooling and shoving each other aside. Chairs and tables were knocked aside in their haste.

One table of people in the back corner remained still. Their faces contorted into a mixture of confusion, curiosity and horror.

"Run!" Kelly screamed at them. "They're going to eat you!"

The people smiled, then slowly started clapping.

They think this is a show.

She tried to help them. What more could she do? She had to save herself.

Kelly and her parents raced for the exit, but as they reached the door, it wouldn't budge. Locked!

Kelly's dad kicked the door, but it didn't do anything. Kelly's mum cried at her husband's side.

In the back of the restaurant, the other family was cornered in much the same way.

"Please," Kelly begged, "You can't eat us!"

Drool dribbled down the pudgy lady's dress as she eyed Kelly hungrily. "If we weren't meant to eat people, why are they made out of delicious, tasty meat?"

The group of cannibals lunged forwards, teeth gnashing and hands grasping for Kelly and her family.

Hopping Around the Prison

Connor stared up at the imposing prison gatehouse before him. A cold shiver ran down his back. Ever since he began researching this place for his school project he had become obsessed with it, and then when he found out it was haunted, he hounded his mum for weeks until she eventually booked them on a tour. It wasn't the scary night tour he wanted to go on because his mum and younger sister, Sarah, were too scared. Still, the proud Western Australian prison was world-renowned for its hauntings. Not only that, rumours floated about that people occasionally went missing on these tours, even the daytime ones.

Connor didn't have to worry about Sarah. If a ghost tried to abduct her, they'd return her within the hour. She's that annoying.

Two large octagonal towers stood either side of a solid wall of limestone, with a large archway leading into the long shutdown gaol. A giant clock face was embedded near the top of a domed wall, and as it struck 11:30am, a bell tolled inside.

"Everyone on the morning tour, please come this way," said a tall tour guide dressed in a prison officer's uniform: navy pants and a light blue shirt. Around his belt hung a set of keys and a walkie talkie.

Connor dragged his mum and sister over to the man and handed him their tickets.

"Go wait inside over there." The tour guide pointed to the prison's new arrival processing room. "I'll be with you shortly." His smile was warm, but his eyes were cold, which made Connor take a step back.

They joined a growing group of people on the same tour. There was a young couple snuggling in the corner of the room, an older couple who were whispering in a language Connor had never heard before, and another family with a toddler and a boy Connor's age.

One of the girls near the door screamed as the prison officer entered the room with a "Boo!" He scowled at her for a moment, and then chuckled. "All right you lot. My name's Eric, and you're about to get locked up in *my* prison."

Sarah stiffened beside Connor and whimpered.

Connor's heart beat a little faster, but he rolled his eyes at his sister. Of course they weren't going to get locked up. It was all part of the theatrics.

The walkie talkie on Eric's belt crackled and he placed it near his ear. A distorted female voice came across the speaker. "No, Eric, these aren't prisoners. They're here for the tour."

"You sure? Okay, Roger that. Over." Eric clipped the walkie talkie back to his belt and appraised the people in the room. "So, none of you are actually here to be locked up?"

Connor shook his head with a small smile.

The female teenager, a skinny girl dressed all in black, pushed her boyfriend forward with a shriek of laughter. "Danny is! Lock him up!"

Eric smiled. "Excellent. And what crime do you wish to confess to?" He marched over to Danny, standing a whole head taller than him. "Huh?"

Danny shrunk down away from Eric, his face turning tomato red. "Uh, nothing."

The girl took several photos of the whole thing, giggling the entire time.

Eric slapped Danny on the back. "You're all right, kid."

Returning to the centre of the room, Eric clapped his hands together. "I guess we should get this party started!" He spent a few minutes discussing the processing unit, the first step in a new or returning prisoner entering jail. Connor's stomach twisted in knots. He couldn't begin to imagine going through this process himself. The prisoners had no privacy, almost no rights. It was horrifying.

Sarah gasped as Eric shared stories about some of the prisoners and why they were imprisoned. Some had committed awful crimes, but others were sentenced to jail for stealing food so their children didn't starve to death.

Connor took a moment to appreciate his life. He sided up to his mum and gave her a hug. She patted him gently on the back.

Connor remained at the head of the group as they left the processing unit behind and stepped out into daylight again.

Before them stood the prison cell blocks. Eric waited for the last stragglers to catch up.

"Do you think we might see a ghost?" Connor asked Eric.

Eric smirked. "You came here for the ghosts, did you?"

Connor nodded.

"You should have come on the night tour."

Connor turned and glared at Sarah. "I wanted to, but someone was too scared."

Eric folded his arms. "You never know. You might get your wish and stay tonight...." Eric inhaled sharply, as if he had said something he didn't mean to. "You said you wanted to see ghosts, hey? Well, seeing them during the day is difficult, but not impossible. Many of the old guards will tell you their stories. If you're in the presence of a ghost, the first thing you'll notice is a coldness wash over you. Then, the hairs on the back of your neck will stand. You might even smell something rotten."

A gust of wind dropped the temperature a few degrees. Connor's arm hairs stood up and he shivered with a grin. "Were you a guard here?"

Eric sighed. "Unfortunately, no. But my father was. I grew up wanting to follow in his footsteps, but the prison was shut down before I could get a job here. The new prisons aren't the same. This place has history," Eric spoke so quietly that only Connor could hear him. "This place has..." his voice faded away.

Connor's mum knelt down beside Sarah. "He's just telling stories, sweetie. There are no ghosts here."

Sarah nodded, but held their mother's hand tightly.

"Okay, now that we're all here, I want to tell you all a bit about the prison." Eric tucked his thumbs into his belt and hefted it up. "This gaol was built between 1851 and 1859 and was closed in 1991 after a significant riot that caused millions of dollars worth of damage. It was decided then that the prison would permanently close, and a new, higher security penitentiary would be used in its stead."

"Why did the prisoners riot?" the old lady asked in a thick accent.

The tour guide shrugged. "They say conditions here were terrible."

Out of the corner of his eye, Connor saw a flash of movement.

"Look Mum, a rabbit." Sarah pointed to the cell block on the far right where a small white rabbit hopped along and burrowed underneath the steel gate.

"Those rabbits are a pain in the neck," Eric muttered. He pulled out a silver dog whistle and blew before stuffing it back in his jacket pocket. Then, he spoke into his walkie talkie. "Janice, it's Eric. I've got an escapee on the southern fence."

A moment of silence preceded a stream of crackling static, then, "Roger that."

The rabbit stopped on the other side of the fence. It almost seemed to be mocking Eric as it bounced up and down on the spot, then, it turned and bounded away to its freedom.

"Are the rabbits a problem?" the other mum in the group asked.

"One rabbit isn't a problem. But two rabbits soon become ten, which soon becomes fifty, and before you know it, the place is overrun with the little guys."

The two teenagers giggled.

Eric scratched his chin. "We, uh, we've got a man who comes and captures them and sells them off as pets."

"Oh, can we get one, Mum?" Sarah asked.

"I don't think a wild rabbit would make a good pet." Connor's mum gave Sarah's hand a gentle squeeze. "Besides, there's more to owning a pet than just playing with it. It's a lot of responsibility. You've got to feed it, clean up after it and all sorts of things." Connor's mum shook her head. "No pets."

Connor puffed out his chest. He had learnt all about them in biology at school. "Rabbits have these little scent glands under their chins and near their private parts that they mark their territory with. Sometimes those glands get blocked and start smelling really bad and you have to clean them." Connor scrunched up his nose and used his hands to demonstrate cleaning an imaginary rabbit's private area.

"Ew. That's gross." Sarah turned to her mum. "On second thought, I think I'll stick to my stuffed animals."

Their mum let out a sigh of relief. "Good idea. Okay, now let's follow the group."

Connor, his mum, and his sister walked briskly to catch up with the group as they headed towards the main cell block. It was a long, quadruple story corridor with cells lining both walls. Eric stopped in front of a restored room that showed what the cells originally looked like.

"Up to eighty men were kept in this cell block. Each man had a cell like this." Eric presented the room like a game show hostess. "It measures one metre by two metres."

"One point two metres by two point one metres," Connor corrected.

His mum tapped him on the shoulder while Eric cleared his throat.

Eric took a deep breath, and resumed talking, slightly louder than before. "So the cells were cramped, and they didn't have toilets until the 1970s. They only had a bucket to relieve themselves which were emptied every few days. You can imagine the smell. Electric lights were only introduced in the 1920s."

His eyes hovered over Connor briefly. It was a look Connor was used to. For some reason, his teachers at school didn't appreciate him correcting them when they made mistakes either.

"Take a moment to wander around and have a look at the cells." Eric ran his hands through his hair and glared at

Connor in annoyance. He pulled out the silver dog whistle from before and twirled it around in his fingers as he walked away from the group.

Connor shrugged it off. He was used to being called a know-it-all. He didn't know everything. That would be silly. No one could know everything. But he did like to know as much as he could, and he absorbed every word his teachers told him at school.

He waited for the elderly couple to shuffle out of the way so he could properly peer into the room. There was barely enough space in the cell to stretch out. Not only was it incredibly cramped, there was no television, no Xbox, no games, nothing. Connor didn't know how to feel. Prisoners had done bad things and there should be consequences for those actions, but how far did the punishment need to go?

"All right." Eric clapped his hands once. "We've got plenty more to see, including the gallows which were in operation from 1889 to 1984. Forty-three men and one woman were hanged here."

"Martha Rendell," Connor whispered.

Eric sighed and put a finger to his lips. "We'll chat more about her soon. She's a very interesting lady and there are still debates now about whether she was innocent or guilty."

At the mention of the gallows, the energy of the group lifted with excited chatter. Connor perked up, he didn't want to miss the gallows. If he was going to see a ghost anywhere, it would probably be in that room. He wouldn't admit it to anyone, but he was a little bit nervous, too, and his heart beat a little faster.

Connor took his time, peering into each room as he slowly followed after the group.

His mum turned around from the end of the corridor. "Come on, Connor. Quickly. You don't want to get left behind."

Sarah tugged on her hand.

"Sarah and I are going to skip the gallows. We'll wait for you outside. Hope you see a ghost!" She and Sarah turned a corner and disappeared.

Connor jogged down the corridor to catch up with the rest of the group, but a scratching sound behind him made him stop dead in his tracks. He shivered and the hairs on his neck stood up. Aware of how alone he was, he turned around, but there was nothing there. He resumed breathing again.

He took a few tentative steps forward, and movement in one of the cells caught his eye. Connor stopped. His skin prickled with nervous energy. This was it. He was going to see a ghost!

The canvas hammock in the corner of the room shook and a rattling sound echoed from underneath it. Then nothing.

Connor hesitated. Maybe he didn't want to come face to face with a ghost after all. Especially all alone like he was now. He stepped backwards.

Behind him, there was a crunching sound, like someone eating crispy chips. Connor whirled around, but there was nothing there.

Upstairs, tiny footsteps echoed on the steel structures.

Connor's legs trembled.

A scratching noise reached his ears from underneath the hammock of the cell in front of him. It sounded like the skeleton from the previous inhabitant was clawing his way out of the floor.

A few seconds later, a small grey bunny hopped out from underneath the hammock and bounded over to Connor. It nestled up against his leg.

The room spun. Connor thought he was going to pass out. It wasn't a ghost. His breathing settled. Just a rabbit. Eric did say they were a problem.

"Aw, you're so cute. Are you scared?" Connor bent down to pick up the ball of white and grey fluff.

The rabbit nestled into his hands and rubbed his chin on Connor's face and arms.

"Are you rubbing your scent glands on me?" Connor asked with a giggle. "Am I yours now? I wish I could keep you, but my mum won't let me."

The place was now dead quiet. Connor started walking towards the exit. His mum would hopefully be on the other side.

But the little rabbit in Connor's hands didn't want to go anywhere. It fidgeted and squirmed in his hands.

"Calm down, little guy. It's okay." Connor scratched it behind the ear.

Connor yelped in pain as the rabbit bit his finger. The bunny nearly worked its way out of his grip, but Connor pressed it firmly against his chest, trying to calm it down.

A trickle of blood oozed from his finger and the rabbit sniffed it. A tiny pink tongue licked at the red liquid.

The rabbit's eyes flashed devil red and its two front teeth retracted. Two sharp fangs replaced the flat chompers that had been there a second ago. It lapped up the blood that oozed out of Connor's finger.

Connor yelled and dropped the rabbit. He ran down the hallway, but only made it halfway.

Movement stirred all around Connor. Beds creaked, walls rumbled and the ground trembled.

"Help!" Connor cried, but it came out like a hoarse whisper.

Red eyes appeared in front of him and above him on every level.

Connor's breaths were fast and hard, yet he felt like he was suffocating.

One bunny hopped forwards, then a second. Soon there was an army of bunnies blocking his path.

He turned to retreat the other way, but there were rabbits behind him too. They were everywhere.

They screeched and their teeth made a chattering sound as they clicked together.

As one, they surged towards Connor.

Connor looked around. There was no escape. He almost tripped over his own feet which were numb with fear.

A cell to his left was open and only occupied by one rabbit. He ducked inside and shooed the angry bunny out, pulling the heavy iron door shut. His muscles strained against the intense weight, and eventually it shifted, shutting with a clank.

The rabbits swarmed in front of his cell door, writhing and clawing their way over one another.

Connor forced himself to take deep breaths. His eyes darted around the tiny room. There was no escaping his literal prison cell. But if he couldn't get out, then they couldn't get in. His mum would soon realise he was missing and they'd come looking for him. He would be fine.

He sat down on the hammock, hands trembling, eyes threatening to spill fat tears.

The iron bars didn't deter the rabbits for long. They used their fangs to begin chewing through the metal which only made their teeth sharper and the rabbits angrier. There were no white bunnies, only grey and black ones.

Connor screamed. "Help! Mum! Sarah! Eric! Someone!"

His finger throbbed where the rabbit had bitten him. The skin around the bite mark had blistered up, and small white hairs had begun to sprout. Connor looked at his finger as if it wasn't his own. His heart jumped up into his throat.

A sudden peace overcame the gnawing, romping mess of rabbits, and they parted as Eric stalked up to the bars of the cell.

"Oh, Eric! Thank you for coming to the rescue. These rabbits are attacking me."

Eric grinned around at the rabbits that were now calm and friendly. They rubbed themselves against Eric's legs and their eyes were no longer red. "What? These rabbits? Attacking you?" He looked perplexed.

Connor stared at his feet. "Well, a few seconds ago they were."

Eric pressed his face up to the bars of the cell and smirked. "I know," he whispered.

"What?" Connor cried.

Eric placed his silver whistle against his lips and blew.

Connor didn't hear a thing, but the rabbits reacted like a call to war. They tore into a frenzy, red eyes glinting and sharp fangs extending from their top jaws.

"I never wanted to be a tour guide. I come from a long line of prison officers. I deserve to be one myself!" Eric smiled down on his rabbits like a proud parent. "And thanks to these little guys, I am."

Connor looked down and noticed the rabbits had almost chewed their way through the bars. His legs were weak with fear. "Eric, please. Calm the rabbits down."

Eric's eyes glazed over. "They said the new prison wasn't a good fit for me. The only job they offered me was to take groups of tourists around here and talk about the history. But it wasn't enough. I needed prisoners to control." He bent down and scooped up one of the rabbits at his feet. As Eric caressed the rabbit, it calmed and its eyes stopped glowing red.

"And then I found the rabbits. I'm not sure what makes them so special, but they obey me. I'm their governor, and they're my staff, well, the grey and black ones are. They keep the weaker white rabbits in line."

Backing into a corner, Connor searched for anything that could help him escape or fend off the army of bunnies. And then he saw his arm...

Connor's whole hand was covered in white hairs, and had begun shrinking to a hideous cross between a human hand and rabbit paw. Screaming, Connor shook his hand, but it remained firmly in place.

"You can't fight it," Eric laughed. "There is no fighting it." He looked down as the rabbits finally broke through the iron door and poured into the cell like a tsunami. "You're my prisoner now."

Naughty or Nice

Jane tried to keep a straight face as her mum mixed the cookie dough. She flipped through the pages of her glossy magazine, occasionally letting out a chuckle. This was going to be good!

When the dough was ready, her mum balled up spoonfuls and placed them on the oven tray, humming along to "Jingle Bells" playing on the radio. She had already made eighty cookies, and this last tray would take the grand total to one hundred.

Carl came into the room. "Mum, those cookies smell so good." He reached out for one, but their mum slapped his hand away.

"You can't have any now, these are for after church."

"But they're perfect right now; hot and gooey. By the time church is over, they'll be cold and crispy."

Their mum put the timer on for eighteen minutes and dusted her hands on her apron. "Jane, I have to get ready. Can you come and do the dishes for me, please?"

"No." Jane replied. She finished her magazine and lay down on the couch, clicking the television on.

"Jane, please," their mum begged with a hitch in her voice. "I don't want to be late and I've still got so much to do."

"I'll do it, Mum," Carl said. He walked into the kitchen and started running the hot water, placing dishes in the sink.

Jane pulled a face and mimed, "I'll do it, Mum." Carl was such a goody two-shoes.

"Thank you, honey. You'll have some nice presents to open from Santa tomorrow. Your sister, I'm not so sure." She raised her voice. "Do you think you're on Santa's naughty or nice list this year, Jane?"

Jane did her best impersonation of a sweet little angel. "Nice, of course, Mummy. I love you so much." Jane swallowed the bile that formed in her throat from being so nice.

Their mum gave Jane an exhausted smile and retreated to the bathroom.

"Why do you do this to mum all the time?" Carl asked. "You're so lazy. She only wants a bit of help around the house."

"I don't have to do anything I don't want to do," Jane replied. "I'm not her slave. She chose to make the cookies for church. I didn't force her to make them." She turned the volume up on the television and scooted over to the Christmas tree.

There were three presents under the tree for her: one from her mum, one from Carl and one from her grandparents. She picked up the light parcel from her grandparents and groaned. "Ugh. Clothes. Why can't they ever buy me something good?" She shook the present from Carl. "What didya get me?"

"Leave the presents alone. You know what Mum said about peeking under the tree." Dishes clanged together as he scrubbed them clean.

"I haven't listened to her before and I'm not about to start listening now."

"But you could end up with a stocking full of coal from Santa," Carl warned.

"Carl, do you know anyone that has ever received coal from Santa?" Jane folded her arms. "No. Do you know why?"

Carl shook his head.

"Because Santa knows that we're not really naughty. It's the technology that makes us selfish, the video games that make us violent, the fathers that leave one night and never come home that make us miserable. Santa knows that we're not to blame. Society is to blame."

Carl rolled his eyes. "Whatever you say, sis."

She carefully undid the sticky tape that held the paper down, revealing an expensive make-up kit. "Aw, Carl, you're so sweet. That's exactly what I wanted." She stuck the paper back down and wondered what that strange feeling was that she was experiencing. Was it remorse? She had heard the word before but never experienced it. Her brother had obviously saved up a lot of his pocket money to buy her that gift. And what had she gotten him? She had wrapped a book from his bookcase. Whatever the feeling was, she shrugged it off. She didn't like it and never wanted to feel it again.

The largest present under the tree was to her from her mum and she desperately wanted to know what it was. Every time she tried to peel the paper away, it started to tear.

"Mum knows you peek at your presents every year," Carl said. "So this year she bought sneakproof paper."

Carl's condescending tone set Jane's teeth on edge. Even though he was two years younger than her, it made Jane angry that he thought he was better than her. How could her mum have raised such an awesome daughter, and then a little know-it-all teacher's pet like Carl?

Jane stood and took her empty glass of water to the sink. She dropped it into the soapy water from a height, splashing water over all the dishes Carl had just painstakingly dried. "Oops. Sorry." Jane giggled to herself and went back to watching TV.

The oven timer beeped and her mum called out from her bedroom, "Can someone get that, please?"

Carl was busy drying a heavy chopping board. "Jane, my hands are full. Can you please take the cookies out?"

Jane looked up from over the top of the couch. "Nah, you can manage. It's character building."

"Just help me out for once in your life." Carl muttered something under his breath, but Jane couldn't make it out as he slammed the wooden board on the kitchen counter. He shut off the oven timer and opened the door. The overwhelming smell of freshly baked cookies wafted towards Jane as her brother removed the tray with a Christmas themed oven mitt.

Their mum's footsteps echoed down the hallway and Jane jumped to her feet and raced into the kitchen. She picked up the chopping board and finished drying it.

Her mum's face lit up as she walked into the room. "Thank you, Jane. Seeing you help out a bit is the best Christmas present I could have asked for."

Carl's mouth hung open and he glared at Jane, but didn't say anything.

"Okay, you two. Go get dressed for church. We've got to leave the house in ten minutes."

***

As the church service came to a close, everyone left the chapel for the community centre for hot drinks and baked goods. Jane rubbed her hands in glee as her mum's famous chocolate chip cookies were handed around with much enthusiasm.

Faces turned sour all around the room as people bit into the salty treats. One old lady at the end of the table spat out her mouthful of cookie and her false teeth flew out her mouth in a shower of spit and crumbs.

Jane struggled to keep her giggling contained, but the sight of the flying dentures made her explode with an unladylike chortle that she tried to conceal as a cough. She ignored the glares from the parishioners.

Her mum was mortified and surreptitiously spat out her half-chewed cookie into a napkin with a grimace. "I am so sorry everyone. I must have accidentally mixed up the salt and sugar." She sniffed, and a few seconds later she was balling her eyes out.

Two of the parishioners came to her side, wrapping comforting arms around her shoulders. One of them said, "Karen, it's okay. Mistakes happen. You've got a lot on your plate."

The other held her hand. "And besides, there's plenty of other treats here." She picked up a gingerbread man and handed it to Jane's mum.

She wiped away the tears, straightening her back. "Thanks." She smiled at them both. "This is the first Christmas without Mark, and I wanted it to be perfect." She started sobbing again. "I'm sorry for ruining your evening. Come on kids, let's go."

Jane hadn't expected her mum to cry like that, but there was no time to feel bad. She jumped to her feet to go home, but Carl grabbed her by the sleeve. He glared at Jane with suspicious eyes.

"No, Mum," Carl said. "We'll stay. We haven't sung carols yet and I know how much that means to you."

Jane returned her brother's glare, wishing that for once he'd keep his big mouth shut.

He smiled proudly, knowing that he had beaten Jane at her own game.

One of the older parishioners beamed at Carl. "Karen, you have such beautiful children. You should be very proud." Her top lip curled slightly as her eyes lingered over Jane.

Jane was tempted to poke her tongue out at the old crone, but knew that she needed to keep up appearances.

Their mum nodded up at her. "Thank you. I am very proud."

The carols droned on for almost an hour and Jane entertained herself by substituting some of the lyrics for ruder versions. She ignored Carl's repeated badgering to sing properly. Fortunately, most of the parishioners were elderly and had bad hearing.

***

The house was dark and quiet when Jane awoke to the jingling of bells and a thud on the roof. Rubbing the sleep out of her eyes, she wondered what was going on. Her brain woke up and she remembered it was Christmas. Bells and noises on the roof could only mean one thing.

Jane pretended that she thought Santa wasn't real, but deep down she believed in him. Her fingers twitched with excitement and she pulled out her phone to take a photo of him to prove to everyone at school that he was real.

She tiptoed down the hallway and peeked around the corner. She couldn't believe her eyes. There he was!

A big, jolly, fat man in a red suit hummed "Santa Claus is Coming to Town" while he pulled toys out of a bottomless sack with 'NICE' stamped on it in big block letters. He straightened and stretched his back before downing the glass of milk that Carl had obviously left out for him. "Okay, that's the good kid done, now for the naughty one." He spun around and locked eyes with Jane.

She froze to the spot, finger hovering above the button that would take his photo.

He lunged at her and grabbed her arm, dragging her towards an empty sack with 'NAUGHTY' printed on the side.

Jane screamed, but it was quickly muffled by Santa's gloved hand pressing over her mouth.

She struggled against him, biting down on the white lining of his glove, but missing his fingers as he held her firm.

"You don't disappoint. You are as naughty as they come," he whispered in her ear.

A bedroom light down the hallway switched on. "Jane? Are you okay?" Her mum's sleepy voice carried through the house.

Jane tried to call out to her mum, but it was no use. Santa was bigger and stronger than she was, and she couldn't get any words out against the gloved hand over her mouth.

"Jane?" Her mother repeated.

The bedroom light switched off and Jane realised with horror that her mum wasn't coming to save her.

Santa stuffed her in his sack with a, "Ho, ho, ho," and she fell into darkness.

The inside of the sack was pitch black and weightless, her body couldn't move. She was stuck with her thoughts, and no way to track the time. It felt like she was in there for all eternity, wondering if she'd ever see light again.

A hand wrapped around her ankle and pulled her out of the sack, dropping her bodily to a cold, hard floor.

She squinted into the bright lights and shivered. It was cold. So cold. Her pyjamas did nothing to keep the chill out of her bones.

Her eyes adjusted and her mouth fell open in shock. She was in the North Pole! She was inside Santa's workshop!

They stood in the middle of a huge warehouse facility with row after row of assembly lines for next year's toy delivery. Elves worked diligently at their stations, building cars and trucks, stuffing teddies, painting doll's faces, and soldering wires inside smart phones. A large digital display took up the majority of one wall and counted down the days, hours and minutes until Christmas next year.

There were twenty or so other kids standing around her, all from various parts of the world and all seeming to be around her age. Some faces were stained from tears underneath red and puffy eyes, whereas the majority were wide eyed in wonderment at the magic all around them. A tall, dark-skinned boy shifted his feet nervously. A red haired, pale girl bounced up and down in excitement.

"I bet you're wondering why you're all here?" Santa asked. "Well, you are my top twenty naughty children of the year. Congratulations." He paused to applaud and Jane wasn't sure if she was meant to join in or not. Was being naughty something to celebrate or was Santa just joking around?

After a few awkward seconds, the kids around her began clapping and cheering, and Jane joined in. Somehow, being naughty had earned her a visit to the North Pole. She grinned from ear to ear, the cold dissolving from her bones. Reaching into her pocket, Jane frowned in dismay. Her phone wasn't there. She must have dropped it when Santa stuffed her into his sack. The kids at school would never believe her without proof.

Santa stopped applauding and sneered at them. "Over the years, the world's population has grown considerably, and about a decade ago, my elves left. They complained about the growing workload and they said I was growing too soft. They said I was giving too many naughty children presents and not enough coal.

"After they left, I had a long hard think about what I was going to do." He paused to scratch his bushy white beard. "Without the elves, Christmas would be no more. They were right, of course. I had grown too soft, so I scoured the world for the naughtiest children and brought them here to my workshop to replace the elves. Instead of giving them coal, they would work off their naughtiness."

Jane looked back at the elves and realised that they weren't elves at all. They were children. Hundreds of children sat at benches, with chains strapped around their ankles. No one smiled, no one cheered and no one sang carols.

Her heart caught in her throat as she realised what Santa was getting at and why she was here. Goosebumps flared along Jane's skin and she jerked backwards, bumping into someone.

Santa beamed at them all. "Children, welcome to your new home. You will work twenty four hours a day, every day, making toys for all the nice children of the world. I have a special blend of cocoa that keeps you warm and energised all day long. No need for rest or sleep! Every year, I send the top twenty hardworking children back home to their families, and bring in new naughty blood. Think of it kind of like military school."

The red haired girl began to cry and Jane was worried that she was about to as well.

"Oh, don't cry, sweetie." Santa said, bending down so that his face was inches away from the girl's. "Your parents won't miss you. They won't even remember you." He stood up and held his hands up to the glass dome overhead. "The North Pole is a magical place. All who reside here are removed from the memory of all who knew them. Until you leave, no one will miss you."

He called their names out one by one and they stepped forward to receive their very own ball and chain and toy assignment.

"Jane Harding," Santa read from his tablet computer.

"Jane, for putting your mum through such a hard year, and teasing your brother relentlessly, you can start by mucking out the reindeers' stables with the other undesirables." Santa handed her a shovel that was smeared with reindeer dung. "Don't worry, after a while you get used to the smell."

Jane stepped forward and flinched as the cool metal pinched around her ankle. A short chain wound its way to a heavy ball of solid iron. She dragged the ball behind her as she walked back to the other children. It weighed a ton and her leg muscles burned from hauling it behind her after just a few steps.

***

Jane hardly recognised herself in the moments she caught her reflection in the ice. Her face was gaunt and her arms were sinewy from all the hard work she had done during the year. Her dirty fingernails were brittle and cracked. The cold had made her lips almost permanently blue, and she had frozen tear tracks burned into her cheeks.

With calloused hands, Jane shovelled scoop after scoop of stinky reindeer dung out of the stable and into a wheelbarrow. The stench had almost become a part of her.

Once the wheelbarrow was nearly overflowing, she hefted it up and wheeled it to the massive factory where the other naughty children were building toys. Her ball and chain rattled behind her.

Jane unloaded her wheelbarrow of dung alongside the other mountains of poop in the steam engine room that powered the North Pole. Three huge fires roared inside the sooty machinery.

The smoke in the air made Jane's eyes water. She was so glad she didn't have to work in here. Poor Bradley and Dominic were covered in black soot and sweating profusely. They were always coughing.

An air raid siren sounded, and Jane's skin prickled with anticipation. This was it. The Christmas Eve call!

Jane had worked hard all year. She had been polite, done everything that had been asked of her and more. There was no way Santa could deny her freedom.

She didn't run to the workshop even though her muscles twitched with excitement. *Good children don't run; they walk.* She opened the door to the workshop and held it open for three other children. They each said, "thank you" as they entered, to which Jane replied with, "you're welcome" and a smile.

Jane stood with perfect posture alongside the other children and waved at a few faces she knew. She wondered if she'd see these people again. Her heart ached for all the others here. Who knew how long they'd remain after she left?

Santa stepped up to a podium in the middle of the room and silence befell the crowd. All eyes turned to him in anticipation of hearing their name being called.

Beneath his white bushy beard, Santa's mouth opened and he addressed the children. "Another Christmas is upon us. The majority of you have been marvellous all year, but unfortunately, only ten can earn their place back in society." Santa surveyed the children, and his gaze lingered over Jane longer than the others.

Jane fidgeted in place. *Jane Harding. Jane Harding. I can't wait to hear my name!*

Santa pulled his tablet from out of his red jacket pocket. "If I say your name, please remain here after everyone returns back to their workstations. The new recruits will take over your responsibilities."

Jane Harding. Jane Harding. Hurry up and say my name!

"Dominic Foster, Sarah Rogers..."

Jane's heart beat faster with every passing name that wasn't hers.

"... and finally, Jane-"

"Yes!" Jane shouted.

The boy next to her nudged her in the ribs. "Shh. Santa said Jane Carter."

Jane's chest tightened. "What?" Her posture slouched. "Sorry, Santa. Did you mean to say Jane Harding?"

Santa clutched his protruding belly as he chuckled. "Oh no, dear. I said Jane Carter."

A tall, blonde girl stepped forward. Heavy bags hung under her eyes and her hair was a frizzy mess around her long face.

"This is so unfair!" Jane screamed. "I worked so hard all year and I *deserve* to go home!" Jane pushed the boy standing next to her out of her way and kicked the wall behind him. "I want to go home!"

"Oh, my," said Santa. "You clearly haven't learnt your lesson at all. One year of good behaviour isn't enough. See, it hasn't changed who you are as a person yet. You would have gone home and resorted back to the spoilt brat you were before I took you." He scratched his beard for a moment, deep in thought. "Ah." He lifted his finger into the air. "I know what'll fix you right up. You can take Dominic's place in the engine room."

Jane collapsed on the floor, sobbing hard. She pounded the cold floorboards with her fist. "This is so unfair," she wailed.

135

All Hallows' Eve

Ella sorted through the racks of Halloween costumes, getting frustrated at the lack of scary outfits. She hated that boys could dress up as whatever they wanted, but it was like an unwritten rule that girls had to go as something cute or pretty. Ella wanted to be horrifying, not sweet.

Someone wearing a white sheet over themself jumped out in front of Ella. "Boo!"

"Ah. You got me," Ella said deadpan. "That's the most realistic ghost costume I've ever seen."

"Really?" Jasmine replied, taking the white sheet off.

Ella's eyes rolled dramatically. "When are you ever going to learn about sarcasm? Come on, let's try on a few things."

Ella stepped out of the change rooms in a killer surgeon's outfit, the green scrubs smeared with bloody handprints and spatters. She almost cried at the sight of Jasmine in a cute yellow and black bumblebee costume. "You can't wear that."

Jasmine looked down at the fluffy outfit. "I know, it'll make me too warm. I want something that will make me look cold so a boy will have to cuddle up to me." Her smile turned to a sneer and she shook her head at Ella's outfit. "The scrubs make you look like a man. You want the boys to notice you."

"We should be dressing up for ourselves, not for boys' attention." Ella folded her arms. "If you want a boyfriend, you should find yourself a boy who likes the real you, not someone you're pretending to be."

Jasmine groaned. "Oh my gosh. I didn't realise I was here with my mum!" Jasmine waved her hands at Ella. "Go on, try on something else."

Next, Ella paraded out as a vampire. A corset gave her a skinny waist, while a high collar made her appear stern. She admired herself in the mirror, imagining what effect adding makeup will have.

"Oh my gosh. Yes! That is so you!" Jasmine cooed. She was dressed in a black cat outfit. Her body was hugged by a black leotard, matched with a bushy tail and a headband with cat's ears. "And this is so me. Great, we're done. Let's go."

"Hold on." Ella's eyes narrowed. "Why do you like my outfit? Is it scary?"

"Yeah, kinda. But you look so much older and all the boys will be staring at you tonight."

Ella sighed. "The scariest things in this whole place are the price tags. Jazzy, how about we keep our old plans of having a movie night tonight. We don't need to go to Scott's party."

"No!" Jasmine choked. "We *have* to go to the party. Scott only invites the *coolest* people in school. If we're there, we'll become the popular kids and everyone will love us."

The look in Jasmine's eyes made Ella wonder if she had only agreed to watch the scary movies to be a good friend. If Jasmine could step outside her comfort zone for one night to be a good friend, Ella could do the same thing.

Ella settled on the vampire outfit and Jasmine had her cat costume gripped in her long, slender fingers. They approached the counter and rang the bell for service. An older lady came through the doorway behind the till. Strands of wispy grey hair poked out from underneath a black witch's hat. The skin on her face was pulled taut into a stern look.

Half-moon glasses sat perched on the bridge of her crooked nose that ended in a hairy wart. A red jewel hung from a black chain around her neck, seemingly pulsating like a beating heart. A name badge read, 'Betty'.

"What can I do for you girls?" she croaked.

"We're just getting these." Jasmine handed over the cat outfit and opened up her purse.

"And what about you, my dear?" Betty's gaze swooped down on Ella, bug eyes magnified behind her glasses.

Ella was entranced by the red jewel at Betty's neck. It seemed to know what she wanted, and promised an answer to Ella's question.

"You don't have anything scarier than these costumes, do you?" Ella asked.

Betty smiled. "Finally. Someone with a real sense of Halloween!" She clapped her hands and the red jewel around her neck shone brighter. "Come with me, child. I'll show you the *special* costumes."

Jasmine's phone vibrated. A quick glance down showed a picture of her mum underneath her name. "It's Mum. You go on. I'll wait for you here." She pressed the phone to her ear. "Hello?"

Betty led Ella to a door at the back of the shop with a label reading "Employees Only'.

"It's so refreshing to have someone come through and not just want to dress like a princess or a cat." She gasped and looked back at Jasmine near the till. "No offence to your friend."

Ella shrugged it off. "Yeah, she's a bit of a scaredy cat." She chuckled at her joke.

Betty unlocked the door and pressed a light switch on the inside wall. A light flickered on and illuminated a small storage unit, bare except for a single rack of costumes. As Ella stepped into the room, a black cat ran in front of her, making her jump. It rubbed itself against Betty's legs.

Ella chewed the inside of her cheek. That didn't bode well. Her grandma had raised her to be a bit superstitious, and a black cat crossing her path meant bad luck.

The rack of costumes held a handful of scary costumes: there was a headless grim reaper, a horrifying clown and various demons and monsters with sharp teeth, exposed wounds and bloodshot eyes.

Ella's eyes widened, all thoughts of the bad luck melting away. "Thank you," she breathed. "This is exactly the sort of thing I was looking for." Her attention was drawn to one of the demon masks. The skin was a pale white—almost grey—and half peeled off, revealing the muscles and sinews beneath. Sharp yellow fangs jutted out of the mouth, the eyes sunken and bloodshot. "This is perfect."

Betty's face lit up in amusement. The cat at her feet purred, almost as if it approved.

Ella matched the mask with a ripped and bloodied white wedding-style gown and admired herself in the mirror. "Betty, thank you so much for showing me this. Halloween is meant to be scary. It's not an excuse for just another lame dress up party."

"I know, dear." Betty scratched behind her cat's ears. "Good girl, Morgana."

"Most people don't even know the history behind Halloween and why we go trick or treating and stuff."

Betty stood and sucked on her teeth. "You know, I wish that people were reminded of the real reason behind Halloween."

"Me too," Ella replied.

Betty leaned in closer to Ella, close enough that Ella could feel the warmth of her breath on her neck. "Do you? Do you wish that everyone could experience a real All Hallows' Eve?"

Ella knew it could never happen. But the idea was kind of cool, and Betty seemed really enthusiastic. "Yeah, that'd be awesome."

Betty straightened and the red jewel around her neck flared a brilliant red. She sighed deeply and smiled. "It would be awesome, wouldn't it?" She grinned, flashing her white teeth. "Okay, let's get you girls sorted and on your way. Make sure you're at the party for the sunset. It's going to be extra special tonight!"

***

A gentle breeze rustled the trees along the dimming street as Ella and Jasmine walked up to Scott's house. The blue sky, tinged with pink and orange, continued to darken as the sun edged closer to the horizon. Small groups of children ran from house to house, trick-or-treating their way around the neighbourhood.

"I'd love to go to America one year for Halloween. They go nuts for it over there. It'd be awesome!" Ella said as a Frankenstein's monster and unravelling mummy ran past.

"I hear their pumpkin spice lattes are really nice over there at this time of year," Jasmine said.

Ella stopped in her tracks and stared at Jasmine. "Sometimes I wonder how we're even friends."

Jasmine pouted. "You love me!"

They hugged then resumed walking. "I guess opposites really do attract."

The music from the party reached them before they saw the house. A pop song with a good beat pulsed through the cool air, drawing them nearer. A few foam tombstones littered the front yard and a large spider web filled the front window with an assortment of plastic tarantulas scattered throughout.

They rang the doorbell and the door opened a minute later. Mr and Mrs Reid stood there dressed as a witch and Count Dracula.

"Velcome to our home." Mr Reid said, circling his arm around his face, covering his mouth with his cape.

"Ooooh, I love your costumes!" Mrs Reid said, following it up with a loud witch cackle.

"Thanks, yours are great too."

"Come on in, everyone's out back," Mr Reid said, dropping the cape and accent.

Ella and Jasmine were ushered inside before being taken outside to where the real party was. Skeletons sat on empty chairs, jack-o-lanterns lit up the yard, bats hung from string from the rafters of the patio and more tombstones, spiders, and cloth ghosts adorned the ground and windows.

"This is so cool!" Ella exclaimed as they walked outside.

They headed over to their group of friends who were huddled around a large bucket of water. A girl with a plastic knife protruding from her back was face first in the water. She flipped her head up, splashing everyone with water, a bright red apple in her mouth.

"Who's next?" Scott asked. "Woah! Is that you Ella? Cool Costume!" His voice rose an octave higher. "Hey, Jasmine." He cleared his throat and his voice returned to normal. "Hey, Jaz."

"Hey, Scott. You look *so* good."

Scott flexed his biceps under his Spartan armour and cape.

Jasmine grinned, and turned to Ella with a cheeky wink.

Ella rolled her eyes. Someone needed to make this party more interesting. An idea flashed through her mind. "I'll have a go bobbing for apples." She took off her mask and handed it to Jasmine.

Kneeling down in front of the bucket, she dunked her head underwater. She bobbed around for a while, then started thrashing wildly. She couldn't get her head out of the water. Firm hands wrapped around her shoulders and tried to pull her out but her head remained underwater. The water muffled the sounds of people screaming her name. Bubbles escaped her mouth.

Eventually, she needed air so she lifted her head out, half laughing, half taking in deep breaths. "Got. You," she managed.

Looking around at the faces, there was a combination of relief and annoyance.

Jasmine slapped her on the arm. "Don't do that, okay?"

Groaning, Ella said, "You're such a wuss. I'm just trying to have a bit of fun."

Jasmine threw the mask back at Ella and pouted. Scott had walked away to talk to Georgia who was dressed in a similar cat outfit.

"You look a bit cold," he said softly as he wrapped an arm around Georgia's shoulders.

Jasmine breathed loudly. "That should have been *me!*" she hissed at Ella.

All the kids at the party stood around in a circle and admired each other's costumes. Ella's chest swelled with pride as hers was by far the scariest. Most of the girls had opted for adorable animals, pretty princesses or fetching fairies. The boys had mostly gone for the zombie or vampire look, with a few superheroes and gladiators here and there.

Ella's thoughts drifted back to Betty from the costume store. She wondered what the old lady was doing. She would be appalled at all the scaredy cats here and their weak costumes.

Food and drink were laid out on the table as the last few rays of sunlight started to disappear. A red punch with floating jelly eyeballs was a favourite. A fruit platter was shaped so that oranges looked like pumpkins and bananas like ghosts. Sausage rolls were decorated with tomato sauce to resemble severed fingers and there was a platter of sandwiches that appeared to have worms inside.

Mr Reid ran around the backyard, lighting more candles and lanterns as the night grew darker. When the sun finally dipped below the horizon, the sky lit up bright red for two whole seconds. Ella spun around with a racing heart. She could almost hear Betty from the costume shop cackling in her ear.

A screech met Ella's ears and she glanced up into the rafters where a colony of fake bats hung upside down. One of the bats twitched and Ella's eyes bulged as she realised they were real. In a large swarm, they fluttered off into the night, screeching as they beat their leathery wings. The once-fake spiders seethed in a crawling mass over the webbing in the windows. Decaying hands punched through the dirt in front of the tombstones, and zombies slowly dragged themselves out of their shallow graves. The skeletons' bones cracked as they stood from their chairs and walked around, and the cloth ghosts floated near the lights like moths.

Jasmine's skin flashed white and Ella shielded her eyes. When she looked back, a silky black cat stood where Ella had moments ago.

Ella stared at her friend. A cat. Jasmine had been turned into a cat!

Everyone at the party had been transformed into their costume. Fairies fluttered around the garden, trying to avoid being eaten by the monsters. Two of the boys that had been dressed as vampires fought over the punch bowl. The contents now looked a lot thicker and darker than it had before.

Ella's breaths came in short bursts. What was going on?

Bile rose in the back of her throat. All the food on the table had changed, too. The sandwiches were writhing full of bugs. Small, half banana ghosts floated around the table and the severed fingers were flopping about like fish out of water.

Ella scooped up Jasmine—the black cat—in her arms and ran to the door, trying to get inside. Mr Reid appeared in front of them out of nowhere.

"Vere do you sink you are going?" he drawled. The tips of his fangs glistened with saliva.

"The, the toilet. I need the toilet." Jasmine took a few steps backwards, trying not to let her panic show on her face.

There was an almighty crash behind them as the punch bowl shattered on the floor. The fight between the two teenage vampires escalated. They switched between their bat and human forms, a blur of leathery wings, sharp fangs and spindly claws. Mr Reid flew off to break them up.

Ella made the most of the opportunity and raced inside, stopping in her tracks as she passed the kitchen.

"Dearie, please come and help an old woman out." A much older looking Mrs Reid stood in front of the oven, her skin a pale green with a blossoming of large warts protruding from her forehead. "There's something in the back of the oven I can't reach. Would you mind reaching in and getting it for me?"

Ella screamed and raced outside with Jasmine safely in her hands. They flew out the front door and it slammed shut behind them.

Standing on the porch, Ella caught her breath. She glanced up and down the street where a small pack of wolves sat on their haunches in the middle of the road, their heads tilted back, howling up at the full moon.

That was the moment Ella realised it wasn't just the people at the party who had turned, it was everyone. She slapped her forehead as she remembered Betty's glowing red necklace, and how she had unintentionally wished this to happen.

Somehow, Betty made this happen. Maybe she was a real witch? *If she did this, maybe she can undo it? I need to find her.*

The Reid's front lawn was a mess. A pile of zombies had clambered out of the dirt and were chasing people around the streets. A swarm of spiders as large as Chihuahuas chased a mother pushing a pram down the sidewalk. Instead of children trick-or-treating door to door, groups of monsters broke into houses and terrified the residents.

A witch's cackle drew Ella's attention to the sky. The witch guided her broomstick downwards and hovered about a foot in the air in front of Ella. Her black corset dress billowed in the wind, but her pointy hat remained fixed in place, as if the wind wouldn't blow it off. "Having fun, Ella?"

"Betty! What have you done?"

"Nothing you didn't wish for!" The red pendant against her neck throbbed a brilliant red.

"This isn't what I wished for. Yes, I wanted a scarier Halloween, and I got it, but now I want everything to be right again." Ella's voice hitched with a sob.

"Right?" Betty's voice was filled with outrage. "My child, *this is* right! This is the way the world is meant to be!" She cackled loudly, making Ella's skin crawl. "This is what All Hallows' Eve is about!" She kicked her broom and sped off.

"Wait!" Ella cried.

The broom slowed, sweeping around in a large arc before returning to the girls. "What?" Betty snapped.

"I was just wondering how you managed to do this? You must be really powerful to have done something as epic as this."

"Well, I guess I am pretty powerful aren't I?" Betty wiped a bit of dust off her shoulder.

Ella soothed the wriggling black cat in her arms. "Just how powerful are you?" Ella asked sweetly.

"Oh, my child, you have no idea!"

"Could you show me? Could you make a bunch of flowers appear out of thin air?"

"Pfft. Anyone can do that." With a flourish of her hand, Betty produced a bouquet of red roses. A flick of the wrist and they went up in flames. Fireflies flew out of her open palm and flittered off into the expanse of night.

"Not bad." Ella nodded. "But I agree, that doesn't require much skill or power. Could you turn the sand I'm standing on into gold?"

Betty grinned and lowered her broom to the ground. She stood and spread her feet apart, extending her arms. She muttered something under her breath and the dirt changed from muddy brown to a lustrous gold colour.

Ella put Jasmine—the black cat—down on the golden soil and applauded. "Wow, you are impressive. But I bet there's something you can't do. I don't think you're the *most* powerful witch in the world."

The red jewel flashed an angry red and Betty's eyes narrowed. "I am the high witch of the International Coven, I am a direct descendant of Lucinda the Great. I have the blood of the Salem witches running through my veins!" A fork of lightning carved its way through the clear sky. She took a steady breath. "What, pray tell, will prove to you that I am the most powerful witch alive today?"

"There's only one thing you can do that will prove it." Ella said, crossing her arms.

"And?" Betty snapped, rolling her hand for Ella to elaborate.

"I bet you're not powerful enough to undo my wish."

"Oh, really? Watch this."

Ella tried to keep her face neutral. She had tricked the witch! Everything was going to be okay.

Betty clapped her hands. Nothing happened.

Ella glanced around. Monsters still ruled the night. She opened her mouth to talk but only a ribbit escaped. She clapped her hand over her mouth. "What?" She wanted to say, but it sounded like another ribbit.

Ribbit. Ribbit.

Jasmine—the black cat—and Betty grew bigger.

No. Ella shrunk.

Everything turned to black until warm hands pulled Ella out of her bundle of clothes.

"Did you really think you could fool me, child?" Betty stroked Ella's back.

Ribbit.

Thrills at Thrillville

Kyle could barely sit still as the sign reading, "Thrillville: Grand Reopening. Five Kilometres Ahead' came into view nestled amongst tall conifers swaying in the breeze. He had begged his parents to take him ever since he saw the advert on the television. And now they were finally going! In minutes, he'd be inside riding all the newly revamped rides.

He only had vague memories of Thrillville. The last time he went was for his friend's eighth birthday party. It closed down a few months later, supposedly because a few people went missing, and remained closed for five years. Then, last summer, an unknown buyer purchased it, and after a year of renovations and updates, it was ready for its grand reopening.

The indicator flickered and Kyle's Dad slowed the car, turning left onto the long paved driveway.

Kyle's heart fell as he saw the number of cars in the lot and people already queuing to get inside. He had hoped that being there early would give him the edge over others. But it didn't matter. He was here! They stood in the line for people who had pre-purchased their tickets, and Kyle laughed at the suckers who were standing in the much longer and slower queues for people buying tickets on the day.

A spotty teenager stalked up and down the queues, handing out park maps. Kyle took one and opened it up, positioning himself so that the wind didn't rip it out of his hands.

"Dad, hold this side."

"Sure," he replied. "So where to first?"

Kyle scanned the map. His finger shot straight to Terrorland with all its adrenaline junkie rides. No way was he going to Cartoon City with all its baby rides, and the queues in Aquatown never got that busy so he could go later. "I wanna do all the roller coasters and the Elevator Drop, Dracula's Revenge, The Decapitator, The Claw of Doom, Demon Falls, and Death Mountain!"

Kyle's mum sucked her teeth. "What about the Baby Dragon Coaster? Or the carousel? They sound like fun."

Kyle groaned. "I'm fourteen now. I can go on all the rides. Not like last time when I couldn't go on any of the good ones."

The girl in front of him turned around and grinned. Kyle pulled a face at her when he recognised who she was, Sally Hanson. She was a goodie two-shoes who liked dobbing on Kyle and his friends when they misbehaved or didn't do their work. She wore a pink tank top and denim jeans and her blonde hair was tied up in pig tails. Kyle thought about introducing her to his mum so they'd both have someone to do the baby rides with.

The large clock on top of the row of ticket booths struck eight and the gates opened. Everyone surged forward and scanned their ticket into the turnstile.

All Kyle wanted to do was sprint off to the first ride and get in line. But he had to wait for the two snails that called themselves his parents. His mum insisted on taking several photos so he quickly posed at the entrance gate and in the main thoroughfare before his mum was finally happy.

"Can we go now?" Kyle snapped, tapping his foot on the ground.

"Yes, yes," his mum replied. "What's the first ride?"

Kyle dragged his parents into the thronging crowd of people headed to Terrorland. "Come on! Before the lines get too long."

"I wish you were this enthusiastic about your schoolwork," his mum said. "You'd be getting straight A's."

Kyle ignored the bait. He wasn't going to start an argument with her today. Well, not yet anyway. After he'd done what he wanted to do, he might say something. They joined the line for The Decapitator. The sign indicated a ten minute wait. That was fine. In peak season, the queue for these rides could reach upwards of two hours.

As they waited their turn, Kyle overheard a group of teenagers slouched against the rails nearby talking about the park.

"...yeah, they had to close down the park years ago because a whole bunch of people mysteriously disappeared."

Kyle had heard the rumours at school but didn't believe them. He wanted to hear what the older boys knew. He edged closer to them, tilting his head to the side.

Sally ran up the ramp and stood behind Kyle in the queue. He hoped she wouldn't see him. "Hey, Kyle. Are you excited for this one?"

"Yeah." Kyle strained to hear what they were saying over Sally's annoying voice.

"I saw you were lining up so I thought I'd ride it again," she said.

Kyle sighed. The teenagers had stopped talking about the old park and had started teasing one of the others about being too scared to ride. He missed what they had to say thanks to Sally. "You've already ridden it, have you?" he asked.

Sally crossed her arms and puffed out her chest. "Yep. And I didn't scream once." She looked down her nose at Kyle. "Are you sure you want to ride it?"

Kyle scoffed at her. "Very funny. Where are your parents?"

"They didn't want to ride it again. They're waiting for me outside. Mum started to feel a little sick."

A tall, lanky guy with greasy, black hair called the next group of people to the platform. The older teenagers stepped up, but the attendant sent them away because they had loose items in their pockets.

"Please, people. Pay attention. No loose items allowed. Empty your pockets and use the lockers provided. Okay, next four, step up."

Kyle's heart raced as fast as he and Sally ran for the gate that would put them in the front seats. Kyle's parents stood behind them.

The tracks vibrated as the car pulled up to the disembarking platform. The passengers were cheering and laughing. One lady wiped her eyes. They got out and the coaster surged up to the loading bay. The gates opened, and just as Kyle was about to step on, the coaster pulsed forwards. The brakes screeched and the coaster held firm.

"Just hang on a second." One of the attendants spoke into a walkie talkie attached to his shoulder. Kyle's parents shared a slightly concerned look.

"Okay, ladies and gents, all good. Hop on!" The greasy haired attendant chewed on the inside of his mouth as he checked their straps. When he tugged on Kyle's strap, the buckle gave way. "Lucky we check these things." He gave Kyle a nervous giggle as he clicked the seatbelt in once more. On the second tug, it didn't budge.

A swarm of butterflies fluttered in Kyle's stomach. He almost wanted to get off; it didn't seem safe. His insides were telling him this was a bad idea, but Sally sat next to him with a beaming smile on her face. She wasn't even holding on. If she could ride it twice, then he could ride it once. If he didn't, she'd tell everyone at school and they'd all laugh at him.

The two attendants flashed each other a thumbs up and the coaster lurched forward. It moved slowly at first, through the dark interior of the building. Rolling through the impenetrable darkness, the coaster stopped suddenly, then plummeted down.

Kyle shrieked. Sally whooped. The coaster zigged and zagged, shot up and plunged down.

Then they exploded out into the light of day, shooting up into the sky. They shot around a vertical loop then a horizontal spiral. They dropped to an almost ninety degree angle and went underground. Kyle ducked his head away from the railing that was going to kill him, but his head missed it by a mile. He had the feeling of being decapitated a further four times by support beams and railings.

Kyle's legs were shaking by the time he stepped off the coaster.

"Are you coming to the Elevator Drop?" Sally asked.

"Yeah, we'll see you over there."

"No, Kyle, you go along with your friend. Your mum and I are going to find a coffee shop and wait for you to finish all these scary rides. That was enough for us." Kyle's dad was hugging his wife tightly. Her face was tinged with green.

Kyle shrugged. "Sure, see ya later!"

He left his parents behind as they entered the Zom.B Coffee shop that backed onto the fenced perimeter of the park. Just behind that was a couple of upturned drums with biohazard warning signs on them. A thick red liquid pooled out of one of the cracked tins, and drained towards the café.

Kyle laughed at the detail the park developers had gone to before he and Sally raced down the path that led from The Decapitator to the Elevator Drop. Their shoes slapped against the concrete as they ran. Just as they reached the line, the attendant was closing the gate.

"Is it just the two of you?" he asked.

"Yeah." Sally nodded, catching her breath.

"Come on," he waved them through and they took their positions inside the giant caged elevator.

"Perfect timing," Kyle cheered.

Soft music played over the speakers as the attendant checked all their restraints. This time, there were no issues. The timer started and Kyle gripped the handles tightly, knuckles turning white. Three, two, one.

Nothing happened.

The attendant furrowed his eyebrows. Kyle loosened his grip on the handles.

Sally giggled. "Wait for it..."

The attendant's face dropped in horror, eyes bulging, mouth open in horror. "Stop the ride!" he screamed.

They shot up into the air. Kyle caught the attendant's face change to laughter in the split second before he vanished out of sight.

Shooting up into the sky, Kyle could barely breathe. Gravity and air resistance pushed down on him so hard. They hit the peak of their flight and he felt like his body would keep going. Then they plummeted to the ground again, leaving his stomach somewhere up there.

It didn't look like they were going to stop; the ground raced up beneath them.

When there should have been an almighty crash of metal upon metal, the brakes screeched and the floor opened up beneath them. They came to an abrupt stop about five metres below the loading platform.

"Woah," Kyle managed to say. "That was intense. I fully thought we were going to die."

Sally was breathless from laughing. "You should have seen your face!" She struggled to unclasp the seatbelt around her. "If we have time later, maybe we can come back?"

"Sure." Kyle stretched his neck. "Where to now?"

Following the signposts to Dracula's Revenge, they noticed the lines were getting longer and longer for all the good rides. The line for Dracula's Revenge was especially long.

Kyle groaned. "This is going to take forever."

"No it won't! My parents are up there!" Sally grabbed Kyle's hand and pulled him past hundreds of people. They passed several signs, from the one hour wait all the way to the ten minute wait. They joined Sally's parents in the queue, ignoring the angry glares from several of the nearby people waiting in line.

"Hello, Kyle. How are you?" Sally's mum said.

"Good thanks, Mrs Hanson. Hi, Mr Hanson." Kyle wiped his hands on his pants.

"Where are your parents?" Mr Hanson asked.

"Mum didn't feel too good after the Decapitator so they're going to meet me at Aquatown later on. Luckily Sally was here, because they wouldn't have let me go on my own."

A few screams and shouts carried through the doorway as an attendant stepped out. The screams died as she closed the door behind her. She was dressed like a vampire, wearing a corset, and her face was painted white. She had two sharp fangs extending down from her top jaw.

She spoke in a thick Romanian accent. "My children are hungry. I require ten more victims." She let out an evil laugh.

Kyle made number nine. He rubbed his hands together. This day was going perfectly. "This is meant to be one of the scariest haunted houses in the world!"

"Do you want to go first?" Sally asked.

Kyle glanced up. There were a group of tourists in front of him and they were using hand signals to try and get Kyle and Sally to go first. Kyle puffed out his chest and took the front position. He'd be the one getting the most scares. Perfect! Kyle welcomed the rush of nervous adrenaline that made his arms and legs feel both heavy and light at the same time.

The attendant lined them up and instructed them all to hold onto the person in front of them.

"Humans have persecuted vampires for too long, and my father, Count Dracula, is after revenge! Good luck making it out of here alive!" The attendant disappeared through a hidden door in the wall, her cackles fading with her.

A heavy door opened, leading Kyle into darkness. He tentatively stepped into the pitch-black room and felt around. His hands brushed up against thick, stringy spider's web. He jumped back and Sally laughed.

"Come on, scaredy cat!"

He realised it wasn't a real spider's web, but material that felt exactly like it. He pushed past it, hearing screams and shouts from behind as the others felt the fake webbing. He bumped into a padded wall and had to use his hands to feel around for the exit. They turned right and then left.

A strobe light flashed and a loud cracking noise sounded all around them. Kyle jumped again and bit back the involuntary yelp that passed his lips. Several people behind him screamed.

The floor beneath them dropped a fraction of an inch, but it gave the impression they were going to fall to their death. Kyle rested a hand on his chest and felt the rapid hammering of his heart underneath his ribcage. He slowed his breathing and forced his legs to keep walking.

Around the corner, a dim light flickered slowly, sporadically illuminating the empty corridor. Darkness. Empty corridor. Darkness. Empty Corridor. Darkness. A skeleton rushed at them from the other end of the hallway.

Kyle knew it was coming but he yelled anyway. Sally's hands wrapped around his sides. He had to admit, she was cooler than he thought she was. Maybe they could be friends... if they survived.

They continued on. Scare after scare. Eventually, there was light at the end of the tunnel.

Kyle thought it was unusual that there was no attendant outside the ride. Normally, there was someone trying to sell them photos and direct them to the exit.

They found their own way out of the ride and located the main thoroughfare, stopping in their tracks. The tourists pushed in front of Kyle to get a better view of the parade.

"Cool, I didn't know they put on shows here. This is awesome."

Thrillville must have spent thousands on the show. Hundreds of actors dressed up as zombies ran around the park scaring people. Across the pathway, one of the actors gnawed on a fake human leg. Fake blood spurted from pretend arteries and chunks of flesh dripped from the actor's mouth.

The zombie twitched and dropped the leg. It bounded towards them.

Kyle raised his hands, ready to applaud, when he recognised the face. A brief apprehension crossed his mind.

"Dad?" Had they asked his dad to play one of the zombies? It didn't make sense.

Kyle's Dad rushed towards them and lunged at one of the tourists who fell backwards and hit his head on the concrete with a crack. Kyle's dad snatched at the tourist's arm and pulled it up to his mouth, biting a big chunk out of his forearm.

Kyle vomited.

The Hansons screamed and grabbed Kyle, running away from danger. The entire park had been infested. Kyle didn't care about the why or the how, he just needed to find his mum, and get out of the park safely.

Running down a concrete path, Kyle's foot squashed a takeaway Zom.B Coffee cup. The remaining dregs of coffee were tinted with the red biohazard ooze Kyle saw earlier. He briefly slowed down to look down at it, right when a small zombie child burst out of the bushes and spurred Kyle and the Hansons on. They ran around the back of the rides, aiming for the front gates. The entrance came into view, but there was a problem. The zombies were there too. They were everywhere. Every entrance and exit, every ride, every shop.

This time, the fear and adrenaline wasn't a fun part of the experience. It gripped his throat and made it harder to breathe. His chest ached not knowing what happened to his dad. *Is Mum okay?*

"There!" Mrs Hanson cried, pointing at one of the gift shops near the entrance.

A group of humans were huddled inside the store. A lady stood by the door, waving them over silently.

Kyle and the Hansons cut across the main thoroughfare and ran up to the door, zombies on their tail.

They just managed to get through and slam the door shut when the zombies' bodies slammed heavily against the door. It shook, but stood strong.

The shop keeper locked the door and put the key back into her pocket. She walked over to the cash register. "That's the only way in or out of the store. We should be safe in here." She picked up the nearby phone and spoke hurriedly into the receiver.

There were only a handful of people in the room. A few scared children, crying for their parents, as well as a few parents, worried about their children. His heart fell when he didn't see his mum in the room. Where was she? Was she safe? Was she one of them? He hoped there was a way to save his dad. What had happened here?

Bile rose in the back of his throat.

Mrs Hanson pulled Kyle into a big family hug. Even though they weren't his family, he felt like he was going to survive this. He was lucky to have bumped into Sally today.

"What do you think is going on?" Mr Hanson asked his wife in a low voice.

"It's the coffee," Kyle said. It all made sense now. "Sally and I left my parents at the Zom.B Coffee place and out the back there were like these huge chemical waste containers that were leaking. I thought it was just a decoration, but what if it wasn't? What if the Zom.B Coffee is actually turning people into zombies?" Kyle sniffed. If that was true, would his parents ever be okay? What would happen to him now?

"Oh, honey." Mrs Hanson knelt down and rested her hand on Kyle's shoulder. "Don't get upset. Everything's going to be fine."

Kyle took a deep breath. Mrs Hanson was right. Everything would be okay. Somehow, there will be a solution to the problem.

As Mrs Hanson stood up, Kyle caught a look on her face he wasn't meant to see. She was scared too. His eyes prickled with hot tears.

Kyle glanced over to the shop attendant, to see if she had any luck on the phone. The handset rested between her shoulder and her ear as she wrote a few things down on a piece of paper. She nodded, and put the pen down. After hanging up the phone, she swallowed a mouthful of coffee.

Zom.B Coffee.

Arachnophobia

Colourful cartoon characters raced across the television screen and Amber laughed as the dog character tried to kill the cat in increasingly imaginative ways. As the show finished, Amber tossed the last few popcorn kernels in her mouth, her eyes glued to the screen. The opening credits of Ocean's Call rolled and Amber set her empty bowl down on the coffee table and turned onto her stomach, propping herself up on her elbows.

A young girl, Aimee, walked along the beach and glanced around to make sure no one was watching before running into the water. Her legs turned into a bright purple tail and she met up with her best friend, Finny, the dolphin. Together, Aimee and Finny investigated why most of the fish by the reef had disappeared. Amber sighed. *Why can't I be like Aimee?*

She is so cool. Amber twisted onto her back and placed a blue cushion behind her head.

Something landed on Amber's chest and scurried down the length of her body. She jumped up and brushed herself off. On the arm of the couch sat a massive Huntsman spider, its hairy fangs clicked together and its front legs almost seemed to wave at her. Amber screamed and backed away from the eight-eyed monster.

Josh jogged into the room. "What's wrong?"

Amber pointed a quivering finger at the spider and her brother let out a laugh.

"Aww, is widdle Amber Wamber scared of the big scawy spider?"

"Shut up, Josh! Kill it! I hate spiders." Amber's voice was high pitched and shaky.

Josh sighed and went into the kitchen. A few seconds later, he returned with a plate and a glass. Placing the glass over the spider, he slid the plate underneath, trapping it.

"What are you doing? I told you to kill it."

Josh straightened and held the plate at arm's distance away from his body. "Why should we kill it? It wasn't hurting anyone. Besides, Huntsmans aren't poisonous and they eat other insects in the house, so they're helpful."

Amber got up and followed Josh at a distance as he took the spider outside. He let it go on the grass and for a minute, it remained still. Then it turned around and raced at them.

Amber spun and ran inside.

Josh pushed past her as she tried to close the door. "Were you going to lock me out there with the spider?"

She slammed the door shut and flicked the lock in place. "Um. No?"

The spider sat there, a few metres away from the door, then turned around and disappeared into the lawn. Amber shivered. *I am never stepping on that grass in bare feet again.*

Amber pointed a trembling finger at the last place she saw the spider. "You should have killed it. That thing is pure evil."

"It was just protecting itself. Just because you're afraid of something, doesn't mean you should kill it."

Rolling her eyes at her older brother, Amber sucked her teeth. "Don't start one of your pacifist rants again."

A dolphin noise sounded from the lounge room and Amber raced back, hoping she hadn't missed too much.

She watched the rest of the show, jumping every now and again at the sensation of phantom spider legs crawling up and down her body. She couldn't sit still, and after the show she had a shower in the hopes it would wash away the prickly feeling. She scrubbed her skin hard under the scalding water until it turned red, but at least she felt better.

A few hours later, while she ate dinner with her parents and brother, her skin crawled again with the invisible spiders.

Putting her knife and fork down, Amber's mum sighed. "Amber, sit still. It looks like you've got ants in your pants."

Amber scratched her wrist. "It feels like it. There was a spider on me earlier and now it feels like I've got hundreds all over me." Just thinking about it made Amber's skin tingle worse.

"Shame," her mum said. "It's horrible the way your mind can play tricks on you. You need to distract yourself. After dinner, go do some homework or read a book. That will help get your mind off the spider and the itching will go away."

Her mum was right. After dinner, Amber typed up her essay for English and the whole time she didn't feel anything.

But as soon as she realised that, the memory of the hairy black spider and those glistening white fangs returned and so did her prickling skin. Scratching her legs and arms for several minutes, she stopped when she noticed a small patch of blood on the top of her thigh. Her fingernails were bloody.

Downstairs, Amber found the first aid kit in the kitchen and was in the process of pulling out a Band-Aid when her mum walked in.

"What are you looking for?" She pulled her floral dressing gown around her and her pink fluffy slippers whispered on the tiles.

"I scratched myself and I need a Band-Aid." Amber showed her mum the scratch and her mum shook her head.

"Okay, I'll put some cream on your arms and legs. That should stop the itching. But seriously, Amber, you need to stop scratching or you'll scratch all your skin off." She massaged cream onto Amber's skin. "You'll have forgotten it all by the morning. Now, go to bed."

"I hope you're right," Amber said. Now more worried about waking up with no skin than the spider crawling on her, Amber fell into a restless sleep.

The next morning, Amber woke up to the sensation of something inside her ear. Sticking her finger inside, she couldn't feel anything. She went to the bathroom and took a cotton bud to her ear. She felt a small sting and removed the bud to find a tiny white spider on the end. Amber screamed. "I hate this house!"

Josh ran into the bathroom, chewing on a piece of toast. "What's going on?"

"There was a spider in my ear. Tell Dad that he better spray the house while I'm at school today. This is beyond a joke." Her whole body quivered.

Josh rolled his eyes and went back to his breakfast.

At least her skin didn't itch anymore. She removed the bandage covering her thigh and the scratch had mostly healed. Her mum was right; it was all in her head.

Amber went to school and over the first few periods, she developed an earache. By lunch time, the pain had intensified and she couldn't concentrate. Sharp stabbing pains assaulted her ear drum and sounds became muffled. Her teacher sent her to see the school nurse.

The nurse picked up her silver tool and turned the light on, examining Amber's ear. "My, my. No wonder you have an earache. It's very red and inflamed. You must have an infection." She motioned towards the bed in the corner of the room. "Lie down and rest. I'll call your mum and have her pick you up to take you to a doctor. You'll likely need antibiotics."

Amber lay down and the nurse left the room. Out of her good ear, Amber heard the nurse talking to her mum over the phone in the other room.

Her ear throbbed in time with her heart beat. With every pound, a surge of pain coursed through her head. A relentless itch developed inside Amber's ear, but try as she might, her finger couldn't relieve it. When she pulled her finger away, there was a tiny strand of white cotton or something attached to her finger. *Maybe this is all because I put the cotton bud in my ear?*

The itching travelled from her ear to behind her eye and the back of her throat. There was a scratchy sensation all throughout her brain. *Mum! Hurry up and take me to the doctors!* The itch in her throat grew worse so she got out of bed and went to the basin.

She picked up a plastic cup and filled it with cool water before taking a sip. The itch subsided for a moment, but then it returned, stronger than before.

Amber stood in front of the mirror and peered down the back of her throat to see what was causing it. A writhing black mass spewed forth from her throat, cascading down from her open mouth. She stared into the sink where hundreds of tiny spiders crawled around the white basin.

Amber screamed, but the noise was muffled by the flow of spiders still streaming out of her mouth. Her heart galloped in her chest and a cold sweat enveloped her.

She watched her reflection in horror as baby spiders escaped out of her ears, dribbled out of her nose and crawled out from the corners of her eyeballs.

Not all the spiders escaped her body. Some remained inside and scurried around. Amber's skin bubbled with movement as they crawled down her arms and across her face.

The nurse called out from the other room. "Are you okay, Amber?"

She tried to call out for help, but the spiders strangled her words. She banged her cup against the basin to create a noise.

"What's going on in there?" The nurse rounded the doorway and stopped dead in her tracks. She dropped her mug of coffee and screamed, before running away. The door slammed as she exited the building.

Tears streamed down her face as Amber collapsed onto the mass of tiny black monsters scurrying across the lino floor. She scratched at her skin, her fingernails raking across her flesh until her strength left her and open sores covered her body. More spiders poured from her wounds.

Tens of thousands of hairy legs brushed against her skin as they began to wrap Amber. Sticky webbing coated her from head to toe. As the little creatures went round and round, Amber's eyes grew heavy and she sank into blackness.

The Never-ending Nightmare

Adrian's bedroom light switched off and his mum's footsteps retreated down the hall.

Julian tiptoed out of his room and peered into his brother's. "Don't forget what I told you," he whispered. "The monster under the bed will eat you alive once you close your eyes if I call her name three times."

Adrian whimpered in his bed, pulling his sheets up to his chin.

"Sally Anne," Julian sang in a quiet voice.

"Please don't," Adrian begged.

"Sally Anne," Julian repeated.

"Mum!" Adrian screamed. "Julian's scaring me again."

"Julian! Leave your brother alone." Her footsteps grew louder as she stormed back towards them.

"Why'd you dob on me? I wasn't going to say her name again, but I guess you deserve it." He ran back to his room, jumping into his bed. "Sally Anne!" he called out.

Adrian shouted from his room. "She's not real, is she mum? She won't really eat me in my sleep?"

Their mum stopped outside Adrian's door and turned his light on. "No sweetie. Your brother is just trying to scare you. Go to sleep. I promise you, Sally Anne, Sir Killsalot, that graveyard ghoul, and any other story your brother tells you are all make believe. Nothing will hurt you in this house."

"Okay, thanks mum." Adrian shuffled about in his bed. "You can turn the light off now," he said.

She flipped Adrian's light off and a few moments later, turned on Julian's.

Julian shielded his eyes and groaned. "What did you do that for? I was sleeping."

His mum raised an eyebrow and pulled her fluffy purple dressing gown around her tighter. "Don't lie to me. I know exactly what you were doing. Leave your brother alone. He's had nightmares these past few nights because of your wild stories."

"But they're not stories." Julian raised his voice, hoping Adrian would hear. "They're true. I've seen them with my own eyes."

"Julian." His mum's tone demanded no more nonsense, and Julian didn't want to risk losing his Xbox for another week.

Julian moved aside so that his mother could sit on the edge of his bed. "What's going on? Why have you started terrorising your brother all of a sudden?"

"Because it's fun," he said, fighting back a grin.

"You think it's fun?" She shook her head. "I don't think Adrian finds it fun at all."

"Yeah, but that's just because he's a baby."

"It doesn't have anything to do with the fact that he's getting all the attention?"

Julian sighed and rolled his eyes, but the truth was, that's exactly why he was doing it. He hated the fact that his parents spent all their time with Adrian, taking him to appointments, checking to see if he was okay. *What about me?* Had his parents forgotten about him?

It was as if his mum read his mind. "Your father and I love you very much. Once Adrian's better, we'll have plenty of time to spend with you. I am really proud of how mature you've been about all this and your father and I have been thinking. We might consider taking you and your brother on a holiday at the end of the year."

Julian's face lit up in excitement.

"But." His mum held up a finger. "You have to show me that you deserve it. Stop teasing your brother. Right now he needs a friend, not someone trying to make his life any more miserable than it already is."

"Okay, I'm sorry," Julian replied. "If we go away, can we go to that hotel with the indoor swimming pool we stayed at last time?"

"Maybe. But only if you're nice to your brother. Now go to sleep and be the good big brother I know you are."

"Goodnight, Mum."

She kissed him on the forehead and left his room, switching his light off as she left.

"Good night, Adrian. I'm sorry for trying to scare you." Julian called out to his brother.

"It's okay." Adrian's sad voice rang out from the other room.

After everything their mum had said, Julian did feel bad about teasing Adrian. He had been through a lot. So many tests and treatments that didn't work. Adrian didn't want to be sick, but he was. And he was always so nice to everyone. Even when he was in pain, he was never mean.

"Hey, Adrian?" Julian called out.

"Yeah?"

"Tomorrow, do you want to take turns playing on my Xbox?"

The excitement in Adrian's voice was evident. "Yeah! Thanks. See you in the morning."

Julian rolled over and snuggled up into his blankets. He promised himself that he would be nicer to his brother from now on and not be jealous of him for getting all of their parents' attention. In actual fact, Julian benefited from it. He was allowed to play a lot more Xbox because his parents were always preoccupied with Adrian.

Julian closed his eyes and fell asleep instantly.

***

Tendrils of white smoke drifted up from the floor and ripped the sheets off Julian's body. Julian screamed, but no noise escaped his mouth.

A small girl with long black hair covering her face rose up on the smoky mist that came from underneath the bed.

"Hello, Julian," the girl whispered. "You called me?" She floated above his bed. Smoky whispers drifted away from her grey dress and wrapped around Julian's wrists and ankles like coils, holding him in place.

"You – you're Sally Anne?"

She giggled. "Of course I am, silly." The cold grip around Julian's limbs tightened. It burned his skin.

"But, I made you up. You aren't real."

"You're funny," she sang. "Your imagination created me. Where's your brother? I'm hungry!" Her grip around his ankles loosened and she floated towards the door.

"No! Please don't. I didn't know you were real. I don't want you to eat my brother."

The temperature in the room dropped. Julian's breath misted in front of his face.

She zoomed in towards Julian, stopping inches away from him. Her dark hair fell in his face, tickling his skin. "But I'm hungry and you promised me food. Who can I eat then? Your Mum? Dad?"

"No one. You can't eat anyone." Julian was on the verge of tears. He willed his body to wake up from this nightmare.

"Well, if I can't eat them, I guess I'll just have to eat you." Dirty hands pushed the hair out of her face and tucked it behind her ears. Pitch-black sunken eyes stared down at Julian lifelessly. She opened her mouth larger than a human should. Like a snake, her jaw dislocated and opened until Julian's whole head could fit inside. She had rows and rows of sharp, tiny, pointed teeth.

The smoky coils around his feet and hands tightened, and he felt his energy being drained from his body. She dove down onto Julian's body and he squeezed his eyes as Sally Anne prepared to eat him whole.

He opened his eyes to find his bedroom was just the way it should be. There was no evidence of Sally Anne and he was still alive – barely. His heart raced in his chest and he was surprised it could still function at that speed. "It was just a nightmare," he said to himself. His skin was covered in a light sweat.

Moonlight filtered through the gaps in the curtains and shadows crept along his walls.

Julian pushed himself out of bed and walked to his bedroom door. His mouth was dry and he had trouble swallowing; he needed a glass of water.

Julian turned the handle on his door, but it wouldn't open. Looking down at the doorhandle, he noticed the burn marks around his wrists. He gasped. Sally Anne *was* real!

The glass of Julian's window shattered inwards and a knight on the back of an armoured horse burst into his bedroom.

Panic rose in Julian's chest. He pressed himself up against his bedroom door. "Sir Killsalot," he squeaked.

"Ah, Julian, my dear friend. How does the night fare for you?"

Clamping his hands over his eyes, Julian muttered under his breath. "You're not real. None of this is real. I'm having a bad dream. Wake up. Wake up. WAKE UP!"

Tentatively, he opened his eyes, and let out a small yelp when Sir Killsalot's horse snorted in his face. The horse was big and black, with maggots and cockroaches crawling in and out of its nose and in its eyes.

Sir Killsalot wore shiny silver armour and his helmet covered a face that Julian hoped he would never have to see.

"I'm sorry to intrude on your evening with the lovely Miss Sally Anne, but she was going to eat you alive and I couldn't stand by and bear witness to such horror. She is terribly impatient. I like to have a bit of fun with my food first."

Julian's heart jumped up into his throat. This was unfolding exactly the way he had told Adrian it would.

Sir Killsalot lifted the visor to his helmet, showing a half-human, half-skull face inside.

Bile burned the back of Julian's throat.

"I'll give you a thirty second head start. Run!"

Julian leaped through his broken window, landing clumsily in the bushes below, nearly rolling his ankle.

Dusting himself off, he took a few painful steps before the adrenaline kicked in. His legs pumped hard as he raced down the street, putting as much distance between him and Sir Killsalot as he could.

The blast of a war horn broke the quiet street, sending a chill through Julian's bones. His legs moved even faster.

Julian ran as fast as he could, screaming on the top of his lungs. "Help me! Please, somebody, help me!"

Not one curtain moved aside or house light flickered on. Julian was on his own.

Julian's bare feet burned, his lungs screamed for air and he had a painful stitch in his side. "Please wake up. I promise I won't tease my brother ever again. Please wake up!" He closed his eyes and rubbed them, but it was no use.

The horse's hooves beat out a similar rhythm to Julian's heart, growing louder and faster by the second. The horse snorted behind him, spraying the back of his neck with spittle.

"You move fast, my boy, but not fast enough." Sir Killsalot's armour jangled and clapped together as he rode.

A searing pain tore through Julian's neck and shoulders and the world spun. No, not the world, his head! Pavement and sky blurred together as his head continued to roll. When it came to a stop, he was facing his body. It collapsed on its knees then fell forwards.

Julian gasped as he woke up standing in front of a cemetery. His hands shot up to his neck and shoulders and he was relieved to find his head firmly attached. There was a moment of confusion before Julian realised his nightmare was still playing out before him. He backpedalled, knowing what lurked in that cemetery.

Turning around, he jogged down the street, but he ended up at the same cemetery. No matter how many times he changed directions, the road only led towards the graveyard.

Steeling himself for what he hoped was the final part of his nightmare, he proceeded towards the burial grounds.

Walking past the creaky iron gate, the hairs on the back of his neck stood up. His breaths came out in sharp bursts, and try as he might, he couldn't get his heart to calm down. He had told Adrian about a haunted cemetery with a ghoul that drank people's blood if they didn't have a golden coin to pay for safe passage. Julian didn't have to check his pockets. He knew that he didn't have any golden coins on him.

A low howl hung in the air. Clouds obscured the night sky, except for a small midnight-black pocket studded with glittering stars. A mist clung to the ground, swirling as Julian's footsteps disturbed the air. Tombstones reached out of the ground, some brand new, others old and crumbling.

Every tombstone read: *Here lies Julian Fischer. 13/04/05 – 26/07/17. Annoying brother. Least favourite son. Loved by none.*

A solitary tear ran down Julian's cheek. He prayed that dealing with the final made-up monster he created to scare Adrian would finally allow him to wake up. Adrian wouldn't know what hit him, he was about to have the best brother in the world.

The mist swirled off to his right. A scraping sound—like nails on a chalkboard—screeched through his bones and made his ears feel like they were going to bleed.

The ghoul loomed out in front of him.

Huge rotten feet with sharp, black claws dug into the ground. A sickly green body reached up from there, ending in a gruesome face with thick, pointy ears. Warts and boils covered his face, oozing something that looked like snot. Long gangly arms with needle-like fingers reached out for Julian.

"Gold coin pleasse," it hissed.

The hairs on Julian's arms stood up and he trembled. "I, I don't have any coins," he stammered.

"Well. I guess I won't go thirssty tonight." The ghoul lunged at Julian who narrowly managed to duck and roll out of its way.

Julian pushed himself to his feet and ran through the maze of tombstones.

The ghoul's claws scratched against the earth as it chased after him.

Julian ran, faster and faster, until his ankle caught on something and he fell down into a freshly dug grave.

The ghoul, Sir Killsalot and Sally Anne gathered at the top of the grave, leering down at him.

"Why haven't I woken up yet?" he cried.

"Oh, sweetie," Sally Anne cooed. "You're not dreaming. And you don't control us anymore. We're free!" She twirled around in a happy dance.

Sir Killsalot's gruff voice contrasted Sally Anne's sickly sweet tones. "You stopped being our master when you went soft, when you promised to stop telling our stories."

"We had to fend for ourselvesss," the ghoul hissed. "We don't want to be forgotten and starve."

Sir Killsalot dismounted his horse and picked up a shovel. He dropped a pile of soil on top of Julian. "Don't worry. We won't forget you. Every night, we'll unbury you and play with you."

"Every night," Sally Anne sang. Her giggle was the last thing Julian heard before the sand cut off his senses.

ACKNOWLEDGMENTS

Many people have helped me get to where I am today, and I want to express my most heartfelt appreciation.

My family has been nothing but supportive from the beginning. Writing is one of most enjoyable and challenging things I've ever done. Thank you for putting up with me and being a huge source of encouragement and reassurance.

A special thank you goes out to all the people who helped me turn my ideas into this finished book. To name a few: Katelyn Barbee, Doreen Weaver, Melion Traverse, Danielle K. Girl, Leah Kessler, and Logan Jones.

ABOUT THE AUTHOR

Matthew lives in Perth, Australia, where he splits his time between writing, working as a physiotherapist, and teaching group fitness classes. Whenever he can, Matthew enjoys travelling the world, particularly to places rich in history and culture.

You can connect with Matthew online:

Facebook: Matthew Dewar Author
Twitter: @WriterDewar
Website: https://matthewdewarauthor.wordpress.com